Open Liner

Alchemy Ink #1

Katherine McIntyre

Acknowledgements

A tattoo shop series has been brewing for ages, so when Rory first appeared all the way back in Joint Penetration, I realized Alchemy Ink was going to come after the Brannon Boys series.

For Open Liner, I owe the biggest thanks to Molly, Ash, and Emily for beta reading this book and making sure August and Drake's story was a good introduction to the Alchemy Ink series.

I also owe a large shout out to my reader group for sharing their love for the Hot Under the Collarverse with me, especially including all the Brannon Boys love that led into this spinoff of the spinoff! A huge thanks as well to Yuko for the cover and to Raeleen Nelson for her sharp editorial skills.

I'm so grateful to my wonderful readers. Every review, every message, every comment helps encourage me to keep writing, to keep creating stories, and I appreciate you all so much.

And as always, a thank you to my caring friends and family for the support and encouragement—I wouldn't be able to do any of this without you.

Contents

Chapter One

August

“We need to break up.”

I stared at my girlfriend of six months from across the booth at the Zodiac Brewery. When had things gone south between us?

“What?” I asked, even though Serena’s statement had been pretty clear. It wasn’t her fault my mind hadn’t caught up yet. I could be forgetful—I’d gone so far as to forget I’d cut up jalapenos earlier before jacking off. It was a fiery experience I never wanted to repeat. But I didn’t think I was dense enough to miss a breakup heading my way. Though, I guess this wouldn’t be the first...or the dozenth time I’d missed the signs.

Serena glanced away, her arms clasped together in front of her. Her dark brown hair was pulled back into a chignon, and her deep chocolate eyes were serious. "Break up, Aug. We're not working anymore."

"Is this about the toothbrush thing?" I asked. I could be a little needy, but I thought leaving a toothbrush over her place wouldn't be a big deal. And some clothes. And a few of my books. And maybe an air fryer, but I liked to cook, and it was one of my favorite new gadgets. I wasn't moving in, but I was at her apartment at least a few times a week, often enough that having some stuff there made sense. Even if I didn't always stay the night because her high-profile lawyer life was crazy.

"You moved way more than a toothbrush into my apartment," she said, arching an eyebrow. "Look, I just...was never really seeking out something this serious when we got together."

"And then our love magically transformed those views?" I broached.

"If that were the case, we wouldn't be breaking up," Serena said. "You're such a great guy—"

I winced. Those words had been on repeat my whole life, with girlfriends and boyfriends alike, right before they dumped my ass. I was nice, I was a good guy, I was sweet.

Yet I wasn't enough.

"Right, right," I said, lifting my hands up. "But you need to go off and spray your wild oats somewhere else."

"I think it's sow," she said.

"Like with a needle and thread? That doesn't make sense." I probably should've been feeling crappier about getting dumped, but no deep feelings of desperation rose up. Which was a sign Serena had made the right call. Man, this really sucked. "Can we still be friends?"

A smile lifted her lips, the tension around her dissipating. "I'd love that, Aug. You're a blast to hang out with."

Just not enough to fall in love with. My stomach squirmed a little, so I tossed back the Leo beer and took a deep breath, then looked up. The starry ceiling of Zodiac Brewery fit the astrology-themed décor, but it was the quality beer that kept people coming back here.

I checked my phone. I started work in a few hours, but I could head over early to avoid drawing this sad breakup lunch out any longer.

"I'm sorry," Serena said again, shifting in her seat, clearly uncomfortable. Me too. "I thought our fling was fun, but it just feels like friendship."

I shook my head. "You don't need to apologize. I'd rather you tell the truth than do something shitty like cheat on me."

"Not my style," Serena said. "I know we had tickets to see that punk show, but if you're still looking to go with someone, I can think of a candidate."

"That punk show," as if the Dropkick Murphys weren't a regular name. Granted, she'd been only going to join me, not because she appreciated the music. "Yeah, if you want to pass them my information, that'd be great."

This was such a relaxed split it was even bothering me. Most of my breakups had at least a few sniffles or teary eyes, but Serena had just been a fun person to hang out with more than someone I'd craved. Yet now I'd be lonely. And I hated being alone. Rory was spending more and more time over Wyatt's, and at any moment he'd be dropping the news that he was moving out.

I plunked some cash on the table for our beers and stood. "I'm going to head out for work early. Keep in touch, okay?"

Serena flashed me a half-smile, sympathy in her eyes. "I will. I'll figure out a time to get your stuff back to you."

"My air fryer?" I asked.

"Definitely your air fryer." She shook her head, her eyes crinkling with her grin. "I've never used that thing in my life."

"You're missing out," I said as I stepped away from the table. "It's revolutionary."

Serena snorted and rose with her arms open to offer a hug. I stepped in because I was a sucker for hugs, even if it stung. No matter how amiable this breakup was, I'd miss spending time with her. Because "we'll stay friends" meant the same as "you can always visit" when someone moved away. Both just meant less of that person in your life.

When we separated, an audible sigh escaped me.

Serena clapped me on the shoulder. "Might not be me, but you're going to find them."

If only.

I attempted a half-hearted smile and tossed a hand up as I turned on my heel to make my exit. The moment I left the air-conditioned embrace of Zodiac Brewery, the bright, hot July sun beat down on me. Not like it bothered me much though. I enjoyed the summertime, sweaty balls and all.

My Subaru awaited me in the parking lot, but my trip out of the restaurant left me feeling more lost than I had wandering in. Serena wasn't wrong—our relationship had been lukewarm for a while—but I hated being alone. And the loneliness was creeping in more than ever with how often Rory was out lately.

At least I knew one place I could go.

I hopped in my car and set off down the road. Within minutes, I'd reached my destination, my mind humming.

Alchemy Ink was a safe haven for me. The familiar logo with the A for the philosopher's stone and script in black on a white background stood out on the sign, and something in me relaxed. I stepped out of my car and ran fingers through my hair, which was getting long enough that I'd need it cut soon.

When I stepped inside, the scent of the incense Rory liked to burn tickled my nose. He was probably already in for his shift, and even though my first tattoo client wasn't until later, I could use the time to catch up on some artwork in my stall. I specialized in watercolor tattoos, and preferred the medium as an artist as well. Even though I had a stream of alternative income from my watercolor pieces, I'd never leave tattooing. Getting to interact with people all the time scratched an itch an isolated artist's life never would.

"What are you doing here so early?" Rory asked, sitting on the checkout counter instead of a seat. He swished his legs back and forth, a ball of constant energy. With his dark hair, tattoos, and lively blue eyes, he drew plenty of attention, but we'd always gelled as friends rather than anything more. "Thought you and Serena had a date?" Rory had been at our place when I left this morning to run errands, though I'd been far more optimistic about my date then.

"We did," I said, plunking onto the couch stationed against the wall for clients. Our waiting room was filled with shelves of knick-knacks. Weird esoteric shit that fit the theme: glass vials alongside leather-bound books with long-winded deep dives into alchemy I'd never bothered to read. "And then she dumped me."

Rory hopped off the counter and closed the distance to sit beside me. He wrapped his arm around my shoulders in a tight hug. "That blows. Can I be honest?"

"Do you have any other setting?" I challenged. I appreciated him, bluntness and all.

"I thought Serena was just one of your friends for like…two months into your relationship," Rory said. "I didn't even know you guys were dating."

"Apparently she felt the same way." I wrinkled my nose and tipped my head back to stare at the ceiling. "I should get 'let's be friends' tattooed on my forehead."

"In Minimalist lettering." Rory snickered. "Nyx will do it. She loves script tattoos."

A laugh escaped me. Nyx loathed script tattoos. Every artist had their preference, and her style was neo-trad or trash polka, depending on the client. "Why can't I find what you have with Wyatt?"

"Back off, bitch. He's mine," Rory teased, a lightness in his eyes.

"I don't want him." I nudged Rory in the shoulder. I'd always been a romantic at heart, a serial monogamist, the total opposite of Rory. And it had gotten me nowhere. "I just don't understand why, out of a row of people, I pick the one I have the least chemistry with."

Rory shrugged. "I think you pick people you're comfortable with. And that's great—that should be a part of things, but if you're not feeling like you're driving on the edge of a cliff and could sail off at any moment, then what are you doing?"

I shook my head. "That sounds terrifying. Hard pass."

As much as Rory went to extremes, I could see what he was saying—that I played it safe. Serena had been funny, pretty, and we had good sex. But there wasn't... more. And I'd been craving more for a long time. Though what was wrong with wanting comfortable? Couldn't I have that and a thrill?

"I was planning on going to Wyatt's tonight, but I could stay home instead, if you want. We could grab some beers and watch a movie."

My heart squeezed tight. I appreciated Rory's offer, but he was still riding new relationship bliss. I didn't want to take that away from him over a relationship I wasn't even devastated over losing, just disappointed. "I'm working late tonight, so don't worry about it. I've got my favorite client in anyway."

"Is it Renegade Granny or Marine Hottie?"

Damn, coming into work had been the right call. If I'd stayed at home, I would've been bummed out, but being here helped lighten my mood.

"Renegade Granny," I said. "We're in the middle of a splashy mermaid on her arm, tits out and all."

"God, I love her," Rory said.

The clients were one of the things I loved most about this job. Getting to share my art with people—on their skin—was a connection I'd always craved. And Owen made sure we only worked with solid people. He wouldn't permit shitheads to come to his business. He always had a saying that if you let one stay, suddenly the whole place stank.

"She's the best. We've got plans for a whole back piece after," I said. Thinking about what we'd discussed made me want to get out my pad and pencils to sketch the basics.

"You've got that look in your eye, like you're about to vomit up some new art piece," Rory said. "Better hustle to the back."

"Vomit up?" I asked. "Way to make it sound nasty."

"Fine, spread your legs and push because you're about to birth some new art." Rory's eyes gleamed with amusement. I flipped him off.

"All right, I'm going to go 'birth some art.'" I pushed up from my slump on the couch. The fact was, I was more distraught over not having someone than missing Serena a mere hour after our breakup, and that was pretty telling. Yet, as with anything, the urge to spill those images and feelings onto the page grew stronger by the second. Art had been a part of my life since I was a kid, and I'd gotten lucky as hell when Owen took me on as an apprentice.

Sure, I might not have the partner I'd been dreaming of, but I had a solid group of friends I wouldn't trade for the world.

For now though, I'd get my feelings out on the page.

Chapter Two

Drake

S erena had asked for weird favors before, but dropping off her ex-boyfriend's shit topped the list.

After a twenty-four shift, I was exhausted as hell and practically dead on my feet, ready to just crash out, but I owed Serena a favor, and she was cashing it in. And I'd rather get this errand done now than after I got cozy at home or prolonged it for my day off. Castillo women weren't to be fucked with, as both of my sisters had proven our entire lives. I'd swung by Wawa for a coffee and chugged it down as I drove to the address she'd provided.

Why couldn't she do this herself? I might be the youngest, but I'd leap to my sister's defense if she'd gotten in trouble with some asshole. From the way she'd talked about the guy she was dating, I hadn't gotten that vibe, so maybe she just didn't want to see him again.

The coffee wasn't doing shit to wake me up, but it helped a little. At least my shift had been relatively chill. I'd been on cooking duty, and Dooley and Jacobs were on cleaning, and they were some of my favorite people to work with. It could've been worse—I could've been on duty with Hannigan. Fucking hated that guy.

I cracked my jaw with a yawn as I turned onto the road where this ex-boyfriend was supposed to live.

At least this offered a change of pace. My life had become so routine, and I couldn't say I loved it. I'd gotten into firefighting thinking the action would keep me engaged, but hell, lately even that had felt same-old, same-old. It didn't help that Serena was a lawyer and Blair was a doctor, so I'd never quite escaped the cycle I'd grown up in.

Every accolade, every step forward had already been achieved by one of them.

I just wanted something that belonged to me.

I pulled up in front of the house and yawned again. Sleep would feel so good. The two boxes she'd asked me to deliver were in my backseat, so I snagged the odd array of shit—an air fryer?—and strode up the chipped walkway.

The slap of my footsteps in my heavy boots echoed loudly in my ears. Maybe I should've changed out of my sweaty Kennett Fire Company shirt, but if I did that, I'd be heading home, and then I'd be passing out in a bed.

The moment I stepped up to the door, my senses went on high alert.

There was a distinctive scent, one I'd faced so many times in my line of work I couldn't shut it off. Smoke.

A loud shout came from inside the house.

Instinct kicked in.

I dropped the boxes on the ground and twisted the knob, finding it unlocked, then shoved my way inside the house. Clouds of black smoke poured from the right.

"Shit, shit, shit." A deep, male voice came from the same direction, and I burst into what was clearly the kitchen to see the glimmer of flames on a stovetop.

"Grab salt," I called out as I yanked my T-shirt up to cover my nose and mouth.

The guy in front of the stovetop glanced at me, blinking. He held a glass of water in his hand.

"Don't throw the water. Use salt." Fuck it. We could discuss later. I marched past him to what looked like a spice rack. The crackle of flames amplified the emergency, as this could quickly expand into a larger fire.

A large iodized salt container lay in front of me. I snagged it, raced back over, and dumped as much as I could over the fire on the stovetop. He let out a shout, and his hand clapped down on my shoulder, but he didn't yank me back.

The flames sputtered, and I tossed more salt onto the remaining flickers.

My shoulders tensed, my arm poised as I prepared to throw more salt if needed. The few glimmers of flames wavered, more choking, black smoke pouring into the kitchen, but then they zapped out, smothered by the salt.

Coughing sounded beside me.

"Open some windows," I said, not stopping my vigilance on the pile of salt on his stovetop that had been a grease fire mere moments ago.

"Okay," he said, followed by coughing splutters. He went over to the opposite side of the room, and a second later, all the windows were open. The fresh air pierced through the smog clinging to the kitchen from the fire. He came to stand beside me and crossed his arms over his chest. "So, who are you?"

A laugh escaped me. Right, I'd just burst into this guy's house and started barking orders. Even though my gaze didn't leave the pile of salt, I answered him. "Drake Castillo."

Silence greeted me.

"Serena's brother," I clarified. "She sent me over with your stuff. Which is scattered in your front yard."

He let out a low whistle and then coughed again. The salt seemed to have done the job, but I'd wait until the open windows cleared out the smoke before we'd start the cleanup.

"Want to have a seat?" he offered, gesturing to the two-seater kitchen table behind us. "I'm August, by the way. I don't know if Serena mentioned me or not."

I maintained a chill expression even though inside I winced. She hadn't. I was aware she had a boyfriend, but the fact she hadn't brought him home said everything. I took a seat, and he dropped into the other one facing me. "Sorry she couldn't drop this shit off herself."

He shrugged. "That's always the case, right? Let's be friends never really means that."

My heart squeezed tight. Shit, I felt like an asshole. Definitely wouldn't be doing this for my sister again.

August let out a laugh. "Sorry, you're just the messenger, who happened to swoop in and save me from myself." His hazel eyes crinkled, and I got my first good look at the guy my sister had been dating. He had tousled blond hair, a well-trimmed short beard, and the type of effortless attractiveness that always made me slow down a few paces.

Damn. Normally, my sister and I had opposite tastes in men, but this guy was straight out of my fantasies. About the same height as me, lanky but muscled, and the black-and-gray tattoos down his arms, the metal hoops along his ears. *Shit.*

I hadn't gotten laid in far too long, but I wouldn't hook up with my sister's ex. It broke every code.

However, looking wasn't a crime. And besides, chances were he was straight.

"I'd offer you something to eat, but my kitchen's a war zone at the moment," he said, running his fingers through his thick hair. The tilt back of his head showcased his Adam's apple, his neck long and slender. Ngh. "How did you know what to do so fast? I was gonna hurl some water on it."

I winced. "I know the temptation to hurl water is high, but that's the last thing to do for a kitchen fire. A fire extinguisher's your best bet, but if you don't have that on hand, salt or baking soda's next." I licked my lips, realizing I hadn't responded to his question. "And yeah, I work for Kennett Fire Company."

August laughed. "I should've guessed from the shirt. Firefighter or admin?"

"Firefighter." The adrenaline of the job had called to me from an early age, and I loved my career, even if life had been a bit rinse and repeat as of late.

"Well, damn. I got lucky then," he said, his voice the sort of bright and rich that stoked my curiosity.

The salt had quenched the fire as far as I could see, and I pushed up from the seat to do one more check. All clear. "I should get your shit off your front lawn. I tossed it the moment I smelled smoke."

"Let me help," August said. "Most of it wasn't anything I was upset about leaving behind."

He rose and started towards the door, and his arm brushed against mine. Sparks rushed through me, and I sucked in a sharp breath.

Clearly, it had been far too long since I'd gotten laid. I was overdue for a hookup. He didn't move away, just strode in time with me, mere inches away. His teeth were white, one slightly crooked that stood out with his lazy smile. He had a carefree air about him for someone whose kitchen had caught on fire, and I liked that a hell of a lot.

"So, what do you do?" I asked, needing to distract myself somehow.

"For work? For fun?" he asked. "I've always found the question so odd. Like, my days don't just surround my job. I've got a steady schedule of cooking, going to shows, and jerking off, but no one wants to hear about that."

"Hot," I drawled without meaning to. I blamed my exhaustion for knocking out my filter.

August lifted his brows. "Glad you think so. Most of the time I get called a weirdo. Thankfully, I'm surrounded by them."

I snorted as I pushed the door open. The fresh air greeted me, and I sucked in a deep inhale. Only a few books and a shirt had escaped the box I'd been carrying, and I scooped them up and passed the box over to him. "Here you go. Unscathed."

"My dinner plans went up in flames—literally—and I need to air out the kitchen. Do you want to grab a burger—on me? As thanks for saving my house. Rory would've killed me."

"Rory?" I asked. Had he moved on from Serena already?

"My roommate," he said. "Though he's been spending more time at his boyfriend's than at home recently." A slight shadow dimmed August's sunshine, his expression falling for a moment, and that struck me in the chest.

"Pining or just lonely?" I asked, my heart thumping a little harder. I had no reason to be invested in his answer, and yet I was.

"Pining over Rory?" August exploded in laughter, leaning forward and slapping his knee. "Oh god. I've got to tell him. He'll die laughing. Nah, just garden-variety loneliness. Breakups will do that to you."

Right. Lord, I wanted to smack myself. I usually wasn't this slow on the uptake, but whenever I finished twenty-fours, I got a little drunk on the sleep deprivation. Yet the idea of inhaling a burger before crashing out was tempting as shit.

"Where were you thinking?" I asked.

"For a burger? Normally Zodiac, but I think I want Red Square Diner right now." August scratched at his stomach, the movement exposing a sliver of skin. The colors of a tattoo crept around the side, and I wanted to know what else he hid. I had a few tattoos myself, the bug hitting early, but finding an artist with the right style for my pieces took time.

"Sure, I'll join," I said. "I just can't make it long. Got a bed calling my name."

"At four in the afternoon?" August wrinkled his nose as he patted down his pockets, the jangle of keys responding. "What are you, eighty?"

I laughed. "Got off twenty-four hours at the firehouse. I'm going to sleep hard."

August's eyes widened. "Shit, man. Do you need a bed? You can rest in mine first."

My mouth watered, and I bit my lower lip so hard I tasted copper to keep from blurting out what leapt into my head. Because not only had I just met the guy, but he was my sister's ex. So I needed to keep my filthy thoughts to myself.

"I'll drive at least," he said. "Is there anything I need to do about the kitchen before we leave? Any precautions?"

I shook my head. "Might want to let your roommate know in case he's stopping back home, but you've got a draft in there, and the fire is out, so that should clear out the residual smoke."

"All right," August said, walking over to his door and locking up. He then jerked a thumb at the bright red Impreza parked in his driveway. "Hop in. I'm taking you out."

I swallowed hard.

This was a bad idea.

A terrible idea.

And yet, I was going anyway.

Chapter Three

August

Getting out of the house had been mission number one.

All my years living on my own, and I'd never set the kitchen on fire, and of course it happened in front of a firefighter. Stroke of luck that turned out to be, because now the fire was out, the kitchen saved, and I was still going to have a delicious dinner.

Red Square Diner was one of my favorite restaurants in town, as I'd always had a soft spot for diners, especially with the odd hours I worked. Sometimes I was starving after a day at Alchemy Ink, and if I got out at eleven at night, this place was always a safe bet.

I turned up the volume in my car when a classic Propaghandi song hit the playlist.

"Shit, I haven't heard these guys in ages," Drake said. "They were one of my first concerts."

"Good taste," I commented, bopping along to the music as I flew down the street.

"Man, it's been too long since I've been to a show," he said with a sigh. Maybe I should invite him to the one I was going to that his sister bailed on when she dumped me. Would that be weird? Probably.

After a few turns, I caught sight of the bright sign for Red Square Diner. It had a classic vibe with wide windows, yellowed lighting, and a tan exterior. I pulled into a spot in the parking lot and shut off the ignition.

I glanced over at Drake beside me, and my skin prickled with awareness. Right, I'd pretty much abducted my ex's brother. He cut a fit figure in his fire company shirt and cargos, definition there that implied he worked out plenty. While he and Serena had the same dark hair and tan skin, his features were more angular than hers. The thick scruff on his chin and piercing brown eyes framed by long lashes added a hint of pretty to his ruggedness. He smelled like sweat, which I happened to love, and damn, I was far too distracted.

"All right," I said, shaking myself out of my stupor. Serena's brother was hotter than I'd expected, but apparently the whole family had good genes. "Let's get in there and order food before I starve."

I exited the car first, and the slam of the door echoed behind me as I sauntered up the walkway. When I entered, I didn't bother waiting, just wandered to my favorite booth on the right side of the diner. It offered a great vantage point to people-watch, and I liked the comfort of having a spot. Me and the crew from Alchemy Ink had visited here many a time.

When I slid into the booth, Drake took the other side.

"I'm assuming you come here often," he said.

"Townie," I said. "This has been a haunt for me for a long while."

"I had a few spots like that in Roxborough," he said, grabbing one of the plastic menus they kept at the table. He flipped through it with a glazed look.

"Too many choices?" I asked. "Go with the bacon cheeseburger, and you won't be disappointed."

"That easy is it?" He flashed me a grin, his white teeth on display, and my pulse sped up. Well, that was inconvenient.

The waitress came over to our table, her curly hair barely held back by an elastic band. "What can I get you?"

"Two bacon cheeseburgers," I ordered. "Tea for me. You a coffee or tea guy?"

"Coffee," Drake said.

"Got it," she replied. "I'll be right back with the drinks."

Drake leaned back in the seat, his hands behind his head, placing those thick forearms on full display. I licked my lips on reflex, my mouth drier.

"So," I said, carding my fingers through my hair. "Sorry for, uh, abducting you, I guess."

His grin widened, a wicked arch to his brows. "Pretty sure this was a dinner invitation."

Was he flirting, or was that throaty tone just how he spoke? Serena had to hit me over the head with her interest because I was shit at picking it up. Everyone at the shop made fun of me for the amount of missed connections or numbers I collected by accident.

"Who did your ink?" Drake asked, his gaze scanning over me. I shifted in my seat. Right, he was looking at my tats.

"My coworkers," I said, lifting the punk sleeve Nyx had been working on. "Trash polka style here, since that's Nyx's specialty, and Owen is designing a back piece for me."

"Wait, are you a tattoo artist?"

I snorted. "I guess that's why people answer the 'what do you do' question. Yeah, I work over at Alchemy Ink."

"No way, I've been eyeing the place up for a while. I'm used to going into the city to different artists, but I wanted to check out the local talent," he said.

I sat up in my seat, already interested. "You've got ink?"

"Not much yet," he admitted.

"Where?" I asked, since none of his tattoos peeked past his sleeves.

He waggled his brows. "That's only getting seen by select people."

Heat rushed through me. The idea of peeling the shirt off him to view the muscles beneath was so tempting. My mouth watered before the ice water dumped in. Serena's brother. He was off-limits, right? Granted, I wasn't sure of the etiquette over dating siblings. Probably frowned upon.

Granted, it wasn't like she was going to fuck him.

The waitress snuck our drinks over, and I began to doctor mine with sugar, swishing the tea bag around, while Drake took a straight-up sip from his black coffee. His lashes fluttered a few times as he savored the first taste. Not helping the filthy direction my imagination was going. I busied myself with a slurp of piping hot tea, which got stuck in my windpipe.

I spluttered, slamming on my chest as I choked for air.

"You okay?" Drake asked, giving me a concerned look.

Heat flushed my cheeks as I caught my breath. "Totally. Just take my word that I'm not usually this much of a mess."

"Hey, no judgment here," he said, his muscled arms still distracting me. "I'd normally make a joke about choking, but I just met you."

"Trust me, tea's not the only thing I've choked on," I teased. Fuck, I loved sucking cock. I had an oral fixation to the extreme, and it had been far too long since I sucked dick.

Drake's eyes widened, and then his gaze fixed on my lips. I licked them on instinct. Bad August. This wasn't what I should be doing.

The waitress swung by with our burgers, thankfully saving me from babbling about dicks. Though more people should. They were great.

I took a huge bite, relief flooding through me along with the delicious flavors. Just because I hated being alone didn't mean I should latch onto the first person to walk my way—or dive into my kitchen to put out a fire. But the competency wasn't a detractor, if I was being honest.

Drake let out a low moan, and I whipped my head up. His long lashes fluttered again, and the look of enjoyment on his features amplified his hotness.

"Damn, these burgers are so good," he said. "I don't know if it's the tiredness speaking, but I could live off these."

"See?" I said. "Told you."

"So, if you're a tattoo artist, what's your style?" he asked between bites.

"Watercolor," I stated. I rolled up my sleeve to show off the skull and crossbones against a splash of ocean I'd gotten done in watercolor style. This had been one of my first tattoos in the city, and I'd gotten addicted.

"Damn, that's pretty," he said, reaching out. His fingers stopped right before touching my skin, and he looked up. "Can I?"

"Yeah, examine away."

His fingers brushed against my skin, and electricity rolled up my spine. My breath hitched. Even with us sitting in opposite seats, his proximity raised the heat in the room, and I shifted in my seat as he skimmed his fingertips across the tattoo on my bicep. He was just checking out the ink, which had been expertly done. That was all.

"Gorgeous," he said. "I'll have to check out your work sometime."

"You can find it walking around town," I said, pride thrumming through me. "I was one of Owen's first recruits when he opened Alchemy Ink. Me, Cas, and Nyx have been there from the start."

"I'm overdue for an appointment," he said. "Maybe I'll come to Alchemy Ink."

Please do. The words didn't escape my lips though, because yeah, while I'd never met Serena's hottie brother while we'd dated, we'd been together for six months and had just broken up. Weird territory, to say the very least.

"Can't visit you at the workplace," I joked. "Otherwise, I'll be labeled an arsonist." I chewed on another bite of my burger, making a concerted effort to focus on that so I didn't fawn over Drake.

"Okay, so explain something to me," he said. "What's the deal with the air fryer?"

I blinked, not expecting the question at all. "Look, I was trying to educate Serena in the ways of good food, and that's my baby. I needed it back." Truth be told, I had far too many kitchen appliances. Every minor thing made its way into my cabinets, from the cast-iron garlic roaster to my fat separator. All useful, even if the assortment spilled off the shelves.

Drake snorted. "Couldn't an oven suffice?"

I placed a hand over my chest with a mock gasp. "How dare. Next you'll be telling me my insta-pot is a fad too."

Drake crooked an eyebrow. "I mean..."

"Why did I kidnap someone so mouthy?" I teased. "You can pry my air fryer out of my cold, dead hands."

"Far be it for me to part you from your precious kitchen appliance," he said. "I was just here to see it safely home."

"After being up for a million hours," I responded. "How are you still upright?"

"Stamina, baby," he responded, a wicked glint in his eyes again. I shifted in the seat, trying to ignore my cock's valiant attempt to stiffen. "For real, I've done these shifts for years. It's old hat. Your body gets used to the stint to an extent."

"Mm, I like sleep far too much," I said, taking the final bites of my burger. "You couldn't pay me to stay up for twenty-four hours. I think it's awesome you found something you love that much, though."

He wrinkled his nose. "Yeah, it's great."

My brows drew together. "That sounds as enthusiastic as a DMV visit."

He snorted. "Nah, I like the work. It's just gotten a little boring as of late."

"Wait, you run into burning buildings and shit, right?" I asked. "Like, the whoosh whoosh with the hose?"

A big laugh exploded from him. "Is that what we're calling it now?"

I shrugged. "Am I wrong? But if that's boring, what the hell do you find exciting?"

He scrubbed at his face. "Calls are always adrenaline-inducing, don't get me wrong. I'm having more of a life-related ennui. Maybe not boring, but like... no room for advancement. Why I'm pouring all this out to a stranger, I have no idea."

"Hey," I countered. "I'm not a stranger. I'm your sister's ex."

"You know that makes it weirder, right?" Still, a smile crept onto his face, and I savored the twinkle in his brown eyes.

"Weird is my specialty."

He let out another laugh, and I reveled in it. This outing with Drake was as unexpected as the fire in my kitchen, but one was far more preferable. Talking with him was easy and comfortable, and he didn't seem to balk at my oddities, which was always a good sign.

However, while I could indulge in this little flare of attraction now, I couldn't see my ex's brother again.

Chapter Four

Drake

I sagged against the kitchen counter at the station, relieved to be back. The Class K fire was annoying enough to deal with and seemed to be a theme of the week for me.

Except this was a restaurant kitchen with a bit more damage in the aftermath.

And I wasn't treated to a burger with a hot guy after.

I rifled a hand through my hair, a different sort of exhaustion slamming in. The post-adrenaline crash after a call hit like nothing else, but it was worth the effort every time.

Mahoney, our chief, swaggered in looking fresh as a daisy. Clearly, he hadn't just been on a call. He was a heavily bearded guy who appeared gruff but was as soft as they came. I'd heard of chiefs from hell in other fire companies, but Mahoney made sure everyone was taken care of here, and I wouldn't even think of going elsewhere. I might've grown up in the city, but over the past few years, Kennett Square had become my home.

"Castillo," he said, striding past me to pour himself a cup of coffee.

"Isn't that going to keep you up this late?" I teased.

He arched a brow at me, the twitch of his lips barely hidden by his beard. "My schedule's fucked anyway. I was hoping to talk to you."

I straightened up from my lean against the chipped counter. "Am I in trouble?"

Mahoney shook his head and waved a hand. "Nah, not at all. This should be easy. Our usual fundraisers aren't pulling in as much as we need."

I placed a hand over my chest. "Oh my word, you mean ancient fish fry and spaghetti dinners aren't drawing the masses?"

He snorted. "That there's the problem. Clearly, we're not reaching the younger crowd, and I'll admit I'm out of touch. In my day, everyone was happy to bring their families to a fish fry."

"Bro, most of the guys here aren't toting around families, and the ones who are would be wrangling their kids the whole time. You need something that's going to engage folks, that's going to draw people in."

Mahoney's eyes glimmered. "Exactly why I want you to run the next fundraiser."

I wrinkled my nose. Damnit. That would be a hell of a lot of extra work on my plate.

"We need upgrades to the kitchen, and the only thing that'll pay for it is a fundraiser." Mahoney batted his lashes at me.

"You need to stop flirting," I teased. "I'm a young, single guy." Mahoney was as straight as they came, had a missus he loved and two college-age kids, but he liked to give me shit. Though, he wasn't wrong about the status of the kitchen. It had definitely seen better years.

Mahoney barked out a laugh and took a sip of coffee. "Right, so I'll put your name on the agenda."

My brain began to whir with ideas, and I hated to admit this was the sort of thing I'd been needing—a new project to sink my teeth into. The idea of putting together something music-related flared strong—my love for punk was unparalleled—but I wasn't sure I had the contacts, time, or venue for a fundraiser of that magnitude. Still, I knew I could do better than a spaghetti dinner. My sisters had both coordinated everything from impeccable baby showers to full-blown galas, but maybe this was a little space I could carve for myself.

"Yeah, okay," I grumbled, as if this wasn't exactly what I'd been looking for.

"Your shift almost up?" Mahoney asked.

"Another hour and then I'm home and crashing out," I said, tapping my fingers against the counter. "Just going to clean the kitchen in the interim."

"Good, you'll see how badly we need this fundraiser." Mahoney smirked and scratched at his chest. "I have the feeling you'll be up to the task." With that, he lumbered out, cup of coffee in hand, heading toward his office. Guaranteed he had shit to catch up on.

I pivoted to the sink and got to work on the dishes. My pulse raced as my brain soaked up all the ideas rushing in at such a breakneck pace. While I got adrenaline from the calls at my job, this was what I'd been missing, this chance to make a mark somewhere.

The only other thing I wanted lay far out of reach.

I'd tried dating when I first started working as a firefighter, but after three boyfriends in a row got sick of my hours and the unpredictability of my job, I stopped trying. Hookups scratched the itch to an extent, but lately I'd been craving more.

Damn shame the last hottie chemistry had flared with was off limits.

August had appeared in a few guilty fantasies, but I kept telling myself thinking about him was harmless. After all, he hadn't given me his number, and I purposefully hadn't asked. We'd hung out for a single evening, one I hadn't wanted to walk away from, and that was it.

"Hey, Castillo, what are you still doing here?" Dooley's loud voice sliced through the quiet.

I paused mid-scrub of another pan and glanced up. Dooley wasn't supposed to arrive for a bit. Then I checked the clock. Damn, five minutes past my shift's end. "Good question." I shook my head, trying to sink back into reality. I'd been daydreaming for way too long, distracted by a guy I never should've even run into, let alone gone to dinner with.

Dooley slapped me on the back, hard enough to sting, on purpose. His teeth flashed with his grin, those light brown eyes twinkling. "I'd be jetting out so fast there'd be scorch marks."

"I think I'll manage at a mosey," I responded, clapping him on the shoulder as hard and equally on purpose. "Hope your shift isn't shit."

"The last few have been exhausting," he complained, pulling a mug down to grab some coffee.

"Tell me about it," I muttered. "Maybe a full moon?"

"It's like folks are drawn to arson a little more every full moon." Dooley leaned against the counter and sipped his coffee, settling in for his shift. Which meant I needed to hightail it out of here.

"All right, man," I said, my feet carrying me toward the door. "See you around."

He lifted his hand in a wave as I hit my locker for my belongings, then headed to my car. Leaving the fire station after a twenty-four always felt like wading through a nebulous dream territory where I was half asleep, half awake. Still, when I settled behind the wheel, my mind burst to life with ideas for the fundraiser the chief had placed on my shoulders.

I set off for home, taking the familiar roads with ease. This was what I'd been craving, a way to prove myself, to stand out. Not that my folks ever gave me shit about my profession, but for fuck's sake, every family gathering, Serena and Blair had some new achievement, and I was just doing the same-old, same-old.

I pulled up in front of my house, a colonial with tan shutters and a slate roof. I'd bought it a few years ago when I decided I'd be a permanent resident of Kennett Square, but even that made me itchy once in a while. When I entered through the front door, the tug in my chest descended again. The place was too big, too empty.

Too devoid of personality. I was a shit decorator.

I headed for my living room and slumped on the couch, needing to sit a beat before passing out upstairs in my bed. The draw of sleeping here was strong, and I'd succumbed quite a few times, even if it was hell on my back.

My phone buzzed, and I tugged it out of my pocket. Serena.

Hey, are you free next Monday?

I thumbed through my calendar, and the date fell on a non-shift day. Still, I wasn't sure what Serena wanted. Never smart to show your hand too early—not with my sisters.

Why? What's going on?

Her text came through immediately.

I've got a ticket for a Dropkick Murphys concert that I can't use. 7pm Monday night.

I typed out a response, my pulse jumping. I'd found out about the concert too late, and I'd missed on getting tickets.

What's the catch?

She shot back a response.

None. I'll drop you the number of the guy with the ticket. Might have to meet him at the event to get it, but I figured you might be interested.

Interested in seeing one of my favorite bands? Hell yes.

I'm in.

Chapter Five

August

"We need to talk" was one of the worst phrases in history.

Coming from my parents made it even worse. I'd already gone through a breakup this month—were they going to break up with me too? Not that I thought I'd show up and Mom and Dad would say, "Hey, Son, we hate you now." We'd always had a rock-solid relationship.

I pulled up in front of their two-story on the outskirts of Kennett, and a wash of memories flooded over me, the way they always did when I returned home. From skinning my knees on the driveway trying to make obstacle courses to the butterfly bushes out front with the flowers I used to make "soup" with that my parents would pretend to choke down, this house was filled with so much happiness I could burst.

My heart thumped hard as I hopped out of my car and headed up the walkway. Maybe they bought a puppy, and that was all they wanted to talk about. I didn't bother knocking, just walked inside.

"Hey," I called out. "You guys in the kitchen?"

"Living room," Mom called back.

I detoured to the left and walked in to find my parents both chilling on the couch, my mom working on one of her knitting projects while my dad read a book on foraging. Both of them had plentiful hobbies in their retirement, and it comforted me to see them sinking into theirs.

"So, a talk?" I asked, shoving my hands in my pockets and rocking back and forth on my feet.

Mom wrinkled her nose, and my stomach dropped. That was her bad news tell.

"So, your dad and I have been trying to figure out some things," she started, then paused. They both glanced to each other.

"The winters have been getting harder," Dad continued for her, placing his book down beside him. "And we've started to look at properties in Florida."

My mind stopped. "To go down to for the winter?"

Mom shook her head, sadness tugging at her expression. "We're going to put our house on the market."

No. My chest sank, and I slumped onto the loveseat. Where was this even coming from? They'd never sought out that Jimmy Buffet life in the past, just the occasional family visits to Grandma and Grandpa. "You're kidding, right? This is some April Fool's prank?"

"You could always come down to Florida with us," Dad offered. "We'd help you relocate."

I couldn't.

My home was Kennett Square. It had always been. I'd built my client following here, my place at Alchemy Ink. Starting over in tattooing, especially in a whole new region, sounded exhausting.

"But we also understand you wanting to stay," Mom said. "A lot of our friends have been moving down there, and a space opened up in one of their communities. It's not that we want to leave you…"

"But you're going to leave me," I said, the sadness washing over me fast and fierce. Both Mom and Dad settled into silence, and none of us spoke for a few minutes. Part of me wanted to lash out like I was a kid, even though I was well aware moving was a normal thing for people to do.

I just didn't think my parents would.

Even though I was an only child, we still celebrated every holiday together, and I stopped at their place to eat dinner with them regularly.

"When did you guys start thinking about this?" I asked, not sure if I even wanted the answer.

"We've been discussing it for six months," Mom said. "I didn't want to bring up a move if we weren't going to go through with it."

Right, because dropping the news on me was better.

I chewed my lower lip, the urge to bolt rising inside me. I couldn't sit here and small talk, not right now. I'd planned on crashing their dinner, but I had somewhere else I could go.

"Do you mind if I take some time and think on all of this?" I asked, restraining my inner temper tantrum. "This is a lot to take in, and… yeah."

Mom swallowed hard, her eyes going glassy. "Of course, sweet boy. I just need you to know nothing in our decision has anything to do with you."

I struggled to wrap my brain around it. We'd been a unit for so long that getting cut out like this stung.

I pushed up from my seat and strode over to offer hugs to each of them, a tight but brief squeeze as my mind reigned with chaos. "I'll talk to you guys soon," I said before heading back out the way I came.

When I reached my car and glanced out at the house, my stomach gave a sour twist. All those soft, watercolor memories were going to be washed away when someone new bought the house. They'd move in and scrub every trace of my childhood from these walls.

Well, fuck. Apparently my parents *had* decided to break up with me. Sort of. Or at least wanted a long-distance relationship.

All that did was make my guts churn. My attempts at finding a partner of my own hadn't gone so great over the years. Guys, girls, they all ended up wanting friendship rather than anything more. Eventually, it was impossible to avoid that I was the common denominator. The forever friend, too boring or chill or whatever was wrong with me that made everyone want something more with someone else.

I drove down the street and made a quick stop at Wawa for a hoagie before continuing my route to Owen's. The plan had been to swing over to movie night after dinner with my folks, but I guess I'd be earlier than everyone else tonight.

Our boss had been hosting movie night at his place on a monthly basis for years, and I'd attended as many as I could. I wasn't even a die-hard horror fan like Nyx, but I came for the camaraderie.

Owen's rustic powder blue two-story came into view, and I slowed down to park behind another familiar car already parked along the front. The first pinpricks of relief fluttered through me at the sight. I hopped out of the car and headed for the side entrance Owen preferred us to use. Something about too many solicitors at the front door, but we didn't question his reasons, just went with what he asked.

My mind still raced as I entered his house, the bag with my dinner in hand. My stomach rumbled, and I hoped maybe I could silence the turmoil in my head with that—even if it wasn't likely.

Owen stood in his kitchen in just a muscle tee and some shorts, which showcased not only his ink but his impressive physique. I wished he were my type, or that I felt something beyond friendship, because whoever landed that silver fox would be the luckiest person on the planet. But like most of my exes, I couldn't make friendship turn into something more, no matter how much I wished it could be.

"You're here early," he said, in the middle of slicing up some veggies for a platter.

"Ugh," I commented, taking a seat at his kitchen table and setting my Italian hoagie out.

"That good, huh?" he said, making a quick detour to the fridge to get out a dip for the tray. He brought a few cheeses and cured meats as well, then began to assemble another platter. The man always had the best spreads, yet another reason I couldn't fathom how Owen was single. And not for lack of trying either, since he dated on the regular.

"I was going to have dinner with my folks, but they dropped the bomb they're planning a relocation to Florida." I took a vengeful bite of my hoagie, a few shreds of lettuce fluttering to the wrapper.

Owen continued cutting the cheese and meats. "That sucks. Do you have a big family network up here?"

And that right there lay the heart of what bothered me so much. I had an aunt and uncle in another state on Dad's side, but Mom was an only child, and with them leaving, I had... well, me.

All their announcement did was hammer home the reality that I wasn't nearly where I wanted to be in my life. I took a few more vicious bites of hoagie, which helped with the churning in my stomach, at least. Food, the cure for everything.

"Nah," I responded in the middle of chewing on some more of my hoagie.

"Trick question," he said, coming over to sit at the kitchen table with me. "You've got all of us at Alchemy. Might not be blood, but we're family."

My heart squeezed tight. This was why the idea of starting over in Florida held no appeal. I could guarantee I'd never find a tattoo shop like this one, with the closeness I'd always craved. "What movie are we watching tonight?"

"Going for a classic with *Army of Darkness*," he said, passing me the small stack of cheese and meat he'd brought over. "Here."

I lifted my brow. "Look like I need more meat?"

He let out a bark of a laugh. "Boy, it looks like you're desperate for it."

I pouted and leaned back in my seat. "You'd think being bisexual I'd have so many more options, but the guys, girls, and nonbinary babes aren't interested."

"Their loss," Owen said, clapping a hand on my shoulder. "You're one of a kind, August Jones."

Warmth filtered through me at Owen's words, even with everything else still in disarray.

"Need any help?" I asked, the urge to distract myself strong. It was that or cry in Owen's kitchen.

"Sure," Owen said, taking pity on me by the soft grin on his lips. "Grab one of the platters and help me take it to the living room. Folks will be arriving soon."

I hopped up and took my crumpled hoagie wrapper with me, disposing of my trash along the way. When I grabbed the platter of veggies, I sucked in a deep breath. I refused to end up alone and eaten by cats. Given that I didn't even have a cat, the likelihood wasn't high. Thankfully, movie night served as a reminder that I did have community here, and I clung to that with all my might right now.

I set the veggie platter on the coffee table and nabbed one of the comfortable seats on the main couch, a nice black leather one. The folks who arrived last struggled to find a seat, especially when one of us was dating someone and brought them along. We only introduced serious dates though, long-term ones. Which, I guess should've been a sign Serena and I weren't meant to last since I hadn't even asked her.

"Heard you got here first." Rory's voice drew my attention.He stepped into the room and plunked onto the couch next to me. "Why so glum, babe?"

I wrinkled my nose, hoping that would mitigate the slight sting to my eyes at admitting the reason out loud. "My folks are moving to Florida."

His expression fell, a rare moment of seriousness from the guy who was perpetually a flirty charmer. He dove onto my lap and wrapped his arms around me in a tight squeeze, and I hugged him back, grateful for his big response, all while I tried to shove mine down.

"Do I need to sabotage the move?" he asked. "I could always poison their realtor."

I snorted and drew back. Rory hopped off my lap but sat glued beside me, our thighs touching. I appreciated the contact right now.

"Nah, no poison needed," I said. "It's just shit news."

"You're telling me," he said. "If my family members tried to move, I'd kidnap them and lock them in our basement until they relented."

My lips quirked. Hearing Rory's response made my own upset feel a bit more reasonable. He was always good like that. "Honestly, while the news would suck no matter what, it hits harder coming right after a breakup."

"Mmk, next time you get a phone number at work, I'll make you call them," Rory said.

"Unlike you, I don't go after shop clients," I teased.

"Thank you for that," Owen muttered, joining us with his cheese and meat tray, along with the crackers for it. "Rory stirred up enough trouble for the entire place."

Rory shrugged. "Harps isn't mad I'm boning her dad. And she doesn't even work at Alchemy anymore."

I rolled my eyes. Rory and Wyatt were perfect together, but the situation had been a bit awkward when Rory had picked him up while piercing his cock. And that Wyatt was our former piercer's dad. Regardless, they'd somehow made it all work.

"What are we watching tonight?" Rory asked.

Owen shot him a flat look. "I told you two hours ago."

Rory waved a hand in front of his face. "And you think I *retain* information? Ha."

"Is Wyatt joining us tonight?" I asked.

Rory shook his head. "Nah, he's taking Harper out for dinner, and as much as I'd love to see her too, we agreed they needed some one-on-one time."

"Damn shame she didn't tag along," Owen said. "I miss seeing her face in the shop."

"Are you going to replace her?" I asked. She'd only been gone a few months, but Rory was taking on too much being the sole piercer at the shop.

"Working on it," he said. "I'm picky though."

"I'd say it's a problem, but you choose good people," I responded.

Owen glanced at his phone. "I'm going to start the movie. Cas was a fifty-fifty, and Nyx and Becky are arriving late." He popped the TV on, and within a few seconds, the familiar opening to *Army of*

Darkness played on the screen. I hadn't seen this movie in ages, but I could appreciate it for the campiness alone.

"You know," Owen said, giving me a glance. "If you need the extra friend time when your folks move, I'm always here."

My chest squeezed tight. "Thanks." He couldn't realize how much that meant to me, because the offer was everything right now. "I'll take you up on it. I'm needy."

"Not as needy as me," Rory said, elbowing me in the side.

"I could give you a run for your money," I responded. It was the primary complaint I'd gotten from significant others my whole life, that I was too codependent, too needy, fell too hard. It's not like I tried—those things were just hard-wired into my personality.

My phone buzzed, and I checked the screen. Serena.

Did you get the number I sent over? My replacement for the concert can pick up the ticket from you there.

A sigh escaped me involuntarily.

Do they want to join me for the concert? I typed out but then untyped it. See? Needy.

No problem. I typed instead. *I'll text them where to meet me at the show.*

Even if going to my favorite band's show alone didn't hold the same appeal.

Chapter Six

Drake

The night of the concert arrived fast. Probably because I had two long shifts beforehand, which sucked any remaining attention I might've devoted to excitement. Those two shifts had been hell. A bunch of folks had collectively decided to commit arson on the same weekend, which meant a lot of mess to handle on our part.

However, I was thrilled to go to the Dropkick concert, even if it was close to a two-hour drive to Asbury Park, New Jersey. The Convention Hall was a venue I'd always wanted to go to, and sure, it was a haul for a weeknight, but I didn't mind. Not like I had anyone waiting for me, and I wanted to chase the spark of excitement that flared in me as I soared up the Jersey Turnpike.

As long as I found the guy with the ticket. Serena had given me the number, and he'd told me he'd text when he got there and wait outside, that he'd be wearing a Flyers cap. Which wasn't as standout as I wanted, given plenty of Philly folks would be there.

I rolled down the window and drank in the cool breeze that arrived with the oncoming night. Adrenaline pumped through my veins, pulsing from the upcoming adventure, from soaring down the highway, from breaking out of the cycle of work and home I'd been stuck in lately. The green and white exit signs flashed by, mine coming closer and closer.

The other cars zoomed around me just as fast, the hum of the other cars tangible in the air. The concert offered the distraction I needed. I'd hit a wall with my plans for the fire station fundraiser, and it churned up a lot of old frustrations.

That Serena had gotten straight A's through school while I scraped by.

That Blair had excelled at sports while I was passable.

Mediocre was all I'd ever be, and I was sick of my status quo.

My exit arrived faster than planned, and I tossed the blinker on as I merged.

All too fast, the sprawl of Asbury Park came into view, the gorgeous murals marking buildings and the glitter of the ocean in the distance. Fuck, how long had it been since I'd gone to the beach? I let out a low whistle and turned down the road to find parking near the convention hall. It cut a mark on the landscape, the brick building accented by pale trim. I jittered as though I'd downed more than a cup of coffee before leaving. I didn't mind going to concerts alone, but I'd feel more secure about it once I got the ticket. Why couldn't Serena have grabbed it herself? I'd have to bug her about that later.

I hopped out of the car and drank in a taste of the salt-soaked air. Being this close to the beach sparked my soul to life and awakened me in a way I'd missed. Not that I was a Jersey Shore for the summer sort of guy—hell, I wasn't even a summer kind of guy—but a sense of gravity settled over me tonight, something I'd been chasing.

I shot a text to the number of the guy I was supposed to meet as I made my way up to the convention hall. The mint-green entrance stood out from farther down the boardwalk, and to my right, the ocean sprawled out before me, dazzling against the hazy, golden evening sun. The last bursts of light gilded the tops of the waves, as soon night would steal it away. I ran fingers through my hair, mussing up the product I'd run through it after my shower.

People streamed in through the doors of the convention hall, but I scanned for folks waiting outside. Several groups clustered around the area, people catching up and talking, and some leaned against the wall of the place.

My gaze stopped on a guy with a Flyers cap, his head tilted down as he stared at his phone. He seemed my age and in shape, wearing a plain black tee and form-fitting jeans. I had on similar attire: a gray tank top, blue flannel, and beat-up jeans along with my shitkickers. I quickened my pace as I cut across the boardwalk in his direction.

And then he looked up.

Our eyes met, and recognition slammed in.

Kind of hard to forget the guy whose kitchen you stopped from burning down.

And the one I'd been guiltily fantasizing about ever since.

Was Serena trying to kill me?

August's eyes crinkled as a huge grin spread across his features, and my heart sped up. "Hey, Drake! What are you doing here?"

I swallowed hard and lifted up my phone, as if that'd somehow explain it. "Looks like you're the guy I'm getting my ticket from."

August tilted his head to the side for a second, and his eyes widened. "No shit. You're the one taking Serena's place?" Strands of his honey-colored hair poked out from under the hat, and the way it accentuated his square jaw made him hotter. The guy had a laid-back vibe I enjoyed far too much, and with his golden, tanned skin, honey-blond hair, and hazel eyes, everything about him felt kissed by the sun.

"Yeah, shit," I said. "We probably should've exchanged names. That would've cleared things up at once."

"Do you want to hang with me at the concert?" August asked and then scrubbed his face with his palms. "I mean, you can do whatever you want with the ticket. I just… don't usually do concerts by myself."

My chest squeezed tight. Was spending more time around August a good idea? No, not in the slightest. But I couldn't turn him down. Not with the slight pleading look in his eyes and the fact I did want to join him for the concert. I flashed him a grin. "What are you waiting for?"

He blinked at me for a moment. "Is that a yes?"

I clapped a hand on his shoulder. "Hell yes. Let's go." I regretted the touch at once. Electricity sparked through my veins, awakening my synapses. August didn't move my hand off though, and I hesitated before pulling it back. The bright smile he gave me in return made my pulse kick.

"I didn't even realize Serena had a Dropkick Murphys ticket," I said as we walked in through the entrance. "I'd been wanting to go to this show."

"Love the band," he said. "Though she wasn't as keen on going. More of a pity acceptance, I think."

I let out a sharp laugh. "Serena's more a swoony acoustics sort of girl."

"This is a far reach from that," August chuckled as we stepped inside.

The convention hall was massive, with a sweeping ceiling, small restaurants, and shops on either side. Footsteps and chatter echoed around us from the crowd funneling toward the concert venue area, the sounds bouncing around the space. This close to August, I caught a whiff of him, all sage and cedar. His body emanated heat, like standing under a patch of sunlight, and I couldn't seem to pull away.

August strode up to the check-in, and I followed close behind. A guy scanned the tickets on his phone, gave us our bands, and we stepped through the gated area.

"Want to go grab a drink?" he asked. "My treat, since I'm forcing you to hang out with me."

"First, off," I responded, "no forcing required. I'm here of my own volition. And secondly, if you keep buying me drinks, you'll have a hard time getting rid of me."

"Oh, good," he said. "Then that's the plan." He flashed me another guileless grin, and damn, I couldn't tell if he flirted or just wanted a friend. Though friends could fuck too.

Bad. Bad idea.

Serena's ex.

Our hands brushed, and a thrill rippled up my spine again. The temptation to reach over and hold his hand was a new one—especially since that hadn't been my MO. Not in a long while.

We headed to the nearest bar and took a seat at the stools. The show wasn't going to start for another half hour, and it'd be awhile before the headliners too. I had to admit, I'd checked out Triple R's work beforehand, a political punk band, and I'd wanted to watch them live.

"Two lagers," August ordered at the bar, leaning over in a way that made his ass pop. Ngh. He had the sort of ass that would steal attention in any room, two round, utterly biteable globes, even with the denim barrier. Fuuuck. Maybe I should've gone for a Grindr hookup instead of a concert.

Except I couldn't deny I was already having fun, and it had everything to do with an adventure and the hottie beside me.

August paid, then passed one of the pints my way.

"I've got us next time," I said, before I could help myself.

"You know that's a binding contract to hang out with me again," he said, a teasing glint in his eyes.

I licked my lips. I wanted that, even if this was a bad idea. "Deal." I took a sip of the lager and let the cool liquid course through me, though it did little to dampen the flames that danced through my insides. Meeting a hot guy at a punk show had been a long-held fantasy of mine. Of picking someone up in the crowd, finding somewhere private afterward, and losing myself in him. As much as I'd gone to shows in the past, that had never worked out. It wasn't as easy as picking up someone in a gay club, where all it took was a look and a nod.

Except now those fantasies spun out of control.

Because I was at a show with a guy my whole body reacted to, who I genuinely liked being around, but at the same time, jumping in on the guy Serena broke things off with… yeah, that would be such a shit move.

Even if I wanted to.

I might've left my bad boy rep back in high school, but I wasn't a shithead. Just… sometimes I made some reckless decisions.

And sometimes I made those reckless decisions on purpose, just to feel alive.

I chugged the rest of my beer to keep myself from staring at August's ass. I got the vibe he wasn't straight, especially from some comments he dropped, but that didn't mean he was interested.

"I need this tonight so damn badly," August muttered as he drank another gulp of beer.

"What's going on?" I asked, my curiosity piqued.

"My folks are moving," he said, leaning back against the bar. He took another swig. "They dropped the news on me a few days ago."

I let out a low whistle. "You guys are close, I take it?"

August's nose wrinkled. "Not like... in an incestuous way, but I spend a lot of time over at their house. Which is now being sold."

The laugh exploded from me. "Didn't assume the incest, but thanks for the clarification." There was something odd about him that I appreciated, his responses both direct and roundabout in the same breath. His mind intrigued me as much as his body, and that was a rarity.

August placed his empty glass on the bar beside mine. "Let's head in. I'm dying to see the openers."

My heart thumped in double-time, and when he stepped past me, his shoulder brushed against mine again. Pure electricity.

I followed him out of the bar, and we made our way into the concert venue, where the darkened room was packed with bodies. The scent of sweat and ozone filtered through, a unique one I always associated with concerts. A large section of the front had filled in, tons of people all ready to wreak havoc in the mosh pit. As much as I wanted to join them, I wouldn't bounce back like I would've ten years ago.

"Mind if we head up here?" August asked, pointing to the farther back section elevated with risers.

"The old guys' section?" I teased.

"If that makes me old, I'll embrace my ancient, weathered years," August said. He peeled up his sleeve to showcase a film on his bicep over what looked like fresh ink. "If someone knocks into me while this is healing, not only will it hurt like a bitch, but I don't want a gash to wreck my new tattoo."

"What is it?" I asked, casting a cursory glance. The figure was hard to tell, since there was some bleed beneath the second skin overtop it.

"A Charmander."

My brows drew together. "You got a Pokemon on you?" My pulse quickened.

"Hey, no tattoo shaming on my watch," he said. "I know some folks, even at my work, get snooty about choices, but I don't judge anyone. It makes me happy, and that's all that matters."

"No, no," I said, pausing beside one of the chairs. I peeled up my pant leg to show him my calf. "No shaming at all."

August let out a surprised laugh. "Bulbasaur? Nice."

I shrugged, even though the coincidence lit sparklers inside me. "I wanted to test the waters with getting inked, and I was a longtime Pokemon fan."

"Here, move in," he said. "We might as well take a spot here."

I shuffled in closer and plunked into one of the seats, which felt a bit lamer than throwing myself into the pit with the rest of the crowd. We could always move around if needed. Yet, when August sat beside me, his arm brushed against mine, and he didn't pull away. Energy rippled through my veins.

Never mind, this was plenty exciting.

"Is everyone ready for a show?" A guy strode onto the stage, and the spotlights zeroed in on him. The crowd erupted in shouts, and I soaked in the passion, the vibration in the air. "I know we're not Dropkick, but hopefully we can tide you over."

The lights brightened on the stage, revealing the setup for Three R's, and the lead singer took his place at the microphone.

"We're gonna kick things off Three R's style. Ready for the revolution?"

A loud roar erupted through the place in response.

My nerves ignited—from the show, from the promise of this night...

And from the man beside me.

Chapter Seven

August

The concert was fucking fantastic.

The openers had been amazing, getting everyone standing and shouting along to their songs, even if we didn't know them. By the time Dropkick Murphys rolled onto the stage, we'd gotten out of our seats and started surging toward the mass of people in the center. I didn't want to get my arm fucked up after getting fresh ink, but I found myself drawn to the energy automatically.

It didn't hurt that Drake was an amazing guy to go with. He got just as into the songs as I did, contributing to the infectious energy of the show. It definitely beat going with Serena, who would've been looking at her phone most of the time and asking when we could leave.

The final strains of "Shipping up to Boston" played through the venue, and the crowd roared.

"Thank you for being a great crew. Good night, New Jersey!" the lead singer of Dropkick Murphys called out.

"Wooo," I called out, throwing a fist in the air. Sweat beaded on my skin, and my shirt was pasted to my chest from jumping around during the show.

"Fuck yeah," Drake yelled. His hair was plastered to his forehead, and his shoulders heaved from exertion. His dark eyes glittered with mischief, his teeth gleaming with his roguish smile. My insides gave a sharp squeeze in response, and I couldn't deny the fluttering that arose. I truly thought I'd never see him again after we parted ways at the diner. After all, for as much as Serena had said we'd be friends, she'd been quiet ever since the breakup, apart from setting this up.

Par for the course.

If all my exes remained friends with me, I'd have an overabundance.

Drake leaned in close, and his lips brushed against my ear. "Oops, sorry."

Heat scorched through me at his proximity, my whole body rousing to life. I hadn't experienced a nuclear reaction to anyone like this in... well, ever. But from the second he showed up at the venue tonight, my heart had been pumping faster.

"What are you doing after?" he asked.

I met his gaze. "Where do you want to go?"

He blinked, as if surprised by my acquiescence, but clearly he underestimated the combination of extroversion and neediness that comprised me as a human being. "The beach is right there, and I've still got a lot of energy to burn." The husky rasp of those last words right by my ear had my cock waking up.

While I doubted he wanted to burn *that* kind of energy with me, the idea of getting on my knees out there and choking on his cock vaulted into my brain and refused to let go. God, it had been so long since I sucked cock. I licked my lips and glanced down. The worn, buttery jeans did a great job at framing his package, and the bulge there wasn't insignificant. Whether it was in my mouth, my hole, I didn't care. Need rose, sharp and fierce, inside me.

When I glanced back up, Drake stared at me, his dark eyes even more intense than before.

"I'm in," I said, even though I was no longer clear what I was in for. Chances were, I imagined the heat percolating between us, the hunger in his expression. I didn't know if he was queer or not, since Serena had kept her family at a distance. Probably another sign she hadn't been serious about us, but I'd missed all the cues.

"Come on," he said, tilting his head in the direction of the exit, where the rest of the crowd was pouring out. He moved with ease, cutting through any open space with a surety to his steps that I envied. I did my best to keep up with him, but I was klutzy on my best day—all fumbles on my long legs. Only thing steady about me were my arms, and thank fuck for that, given my career.

We hit a few bottlenecks in the crowd, since everyone rushed to get home en masse. I wasn't aiming to hit the road though. No, I wanted to spend any extra time Drake was willing to offer me. It was a good thing I hadn't met him while Serena and I were dating, because holy fuck, he was scorchingly hot. My gaze was glued on his muscular, defined ass, even though I wanted to get fucked something fierce.

When we broke out of the venue, I sucked in a long, lusty breath of the salt air.

And promptly choked on it.

I spluttered, smacking my chest as I gasped out for air.

"You okay there?" Drake teased, a smugness to his tone.

"Totally fine. That's just how I breathe," I proclaimed loftily.

His eyes twinkled as we strolled down the boardwalk. "Right. Completely normal."

I nudged his shoulder with mine in retaliation. Instead, the zing from our connection rocketed through my body, heightening my awareness of the drop-dead gorgeous guy who strode beside me. Damn, he was all hard muscle. I had a little from being active with hiking and shit, but not like... firefighter muscle. My mouth dried at the thought of what he'd look like beneath that tight shirt and weathered jeans.

Damn, I shouldn't be this hard-up for him. It wasn't that long since I'd had sex... with his sister. I winced and looked up at the sky. The late-night stretch of the velvet horizon captivated me, studded with silvery stars and a glowing crescent moon.

"Thanks for inviting me to join you," Drake said, breaking through the quiet that had settled between us. Some folks from the concert strode past us along this stretch of the boardwalk, but most people had made a beeline for their cars. "I didn't realize how few invites I get nowadays."

"Mmm, don't tempt me," I said. "I've got your number now."

"That a threat?" he teased. "Bring it, babe."

The term of endearment sent a flush of heat through me, and when I glanced to meet his eyes, his smirk amplified it to an inferno. Being around him was exciting in a way I didn't feel often, though it was more the adrenaline from the concert and less of the "oh fuck my house is on fire" kind of panic. "You have no idea what you've unleashed. I'm the asshole who sends the daily texts."

Drake shrugged. "As long as you don't mind if I don't always have immediate answers, I'm good with that."

My heart thudded a little harder. That had been a sticking point in my relationship with Serena. She felt guilty because I sent a barrage of messages, and the onslaught was a bit too much for her to handle. Story of my life. If I toned myself down, I ended up bursting, and that wasn't good for anyone either.

"Come on, let's get down to the sand," Drake said, veering to the left, where the ocean glittered nearby. The crash of the waves soothed my soul in a way little else did, and combined with the crisp, salty nighttime air, I was more aware of everything around me. Hard not to be when Drake was so close, the mix of sweat and leather coming from him was intoxicating. He lit me up like kerosene to my system, and I was one match away from an inferno.

The second we hit the sand, I plopped down and yanked my boots off. No way was I doing the drive back with shoes full of sand.

"Shit, that's a good idea." Drake thumped down beside me and began to unlace his big-ass steel-toed boots. I burrowed my feet in the sand, now cooled from the descent of night. Still felt amazing though.

"Did you ever eat sand as a kid?" I asked, staring at it.

Drake burst out laughing, the sound echoing through the quiet between us. "Like on purpose? Fuck no. What the fuck sort of question is that?"

I lifted a handful of it up and watched the grains fall through my fingers. "The texture felt so good I thought it would be equally good in my mouth."

Drake flung himself back on the ground, full-out cackling. A smile rose to my own lips, because I'd done a lot of weird shit as a kid, and that hadn't abated much as I'd grown. He slapped a palm to his chest, which was heaving from laughter.

"Oh god," he gasped. "I haven't laughed that hard in ages."

I mimicked a seated curtsy. "Happy to be of service."

"You're fascinating, you know that?" he said, giving me the side eye.

"Like in a bug under a microscope way?" I asked, running my not-sandy-hand through my hair. I'd learned some lessons at least.

"Nah, like in a strikes my curiosity way," he responded, his voice growing deeper, huskier. The way he looked sprawled out on the sand was sinful. The moonlight highlighted the sharp arch of his nose, his defined chin, those thick brows. I let out a breath I hadn't even realized was trapped.

Damn, I just wanted to climb on top of him and ride. My cock woke the hell up at the thought, and I shifted in my seat, hoping he didn't notice the semi pressing against my jeans. "Well, good. I need a concert buddy anyway."

"If you're serious, I'll take you up on that," he said. "I need to get out to shows more."

"I'm very serious," I said, even though my nose wrinkled. Chances were, I'd get overeager, and he'd get sick of me. Wouldn't be the first time. In the distance, the silhouette of the pier beckoned, dark waves crashing around it. A burst of energy filtered through my veins, pushing me to move, move, move. "Want to walk down there?"

"The pier?" he said. "Yeah, let's go."

I pushed up from my spot on the sand and snagged my boots. The feel of the cool sand between my toes was immaculate, a hit of dopamine I craved. The moon cast delicate lavender beams, the pale sand contrasting with the glittering blackened expanse of the ocean crashing to the shore beside us. Drake kept up with ease as we walked along the beach toward the pier.

The swing of his boots in his hand drew my attention, same with the fluid motion of his arms and legs, as he strolled with me. My gaze snagged on the tight fit of his jeans and the bulge there. Ngh. Damn, he probably had a delicious cock. The adrenaline from the show hadn't crashed yet, and the jittery anticipation filtered through me, flooding my body from head to toe. Not like it would go anywhere. Better to get the energy out with this walk.

My foot snagged, and I vaulted forward. Hands wrapped around my waist, but my arms had shot out, and I was already flailing. My arm knocked into Drake, and our weight shifted.

Down we went.

My back thudded against the sand, which broke most of my fall, and Drake landed with a thump on top of me. The breath knocked out of my chest, and not just from the weight. With his hard, muscular body pressed against me, and his face mere inches from mine, I couldn't pop the lid on the attraction that had been bubbling under the surface from the moment we met.

His dark eyes burned with heat, muscular arms bracketed me on either side, his hands pressed into the sand, but he didn't budge. My thigh nudged against his groin, and I shifted slightly. Oh fuck, he was hard. A thrill shot through me, and I swallowed hard. Drake stared at me, not looking away.

"You're trouble, August," he murmured, his voice hoarse and raspy.

"Is that a bad thing?" I asked, my breath coming in a little faster. God, I wanted to close the distance between us, to taste those lips. His were carved and perfect, and his hot breath puffed against my face. Fuck. I didn't want to move. Didn't want to leave this space where he was pressed against me, his intoxicating scent of sweat and musk captivating.

I tilted upward on automatic, as if those inches between us could magically disappear.

His gaze zeroed in on my mouth, and my breath hitched.

A universe spanned between us, impossible to cross, yet we were close enough that our breaths mingled. The tension increased to the point I could've sworn it buzzed in the air, and I licked my lips, which had grown dry with anticipation.

Drake's eyes widened, and that was it.

With the suddenness of thunder, we were colliding, our lips crashing together.

I wasn't sure who'd initiated the kiss, if it was him, or if it was me, but it didn't matter. His mouth on mine transmuted my soul, like the first dip of a wet paintbrush into my watercolor palette. And his brushstrokes were masterful as he kissed me with a fervor that left me breathless and panting. The colors exploded between us, vibrant and evocative as I met him kiss for kiss. His tongue swept into my mouth as he devoured me with a consuming hunger that coursed through my body.

My cells vibrated from this awakening, bursting with life from head to toe. The cool sand against my back contrasted with the heat of our bodies pressed together, and his cock plumped up against my leg, testing the denim it was trapped behind. The feel of his desire sent me reeling, my own need ratcheting up. My length thickened, my balls giving a needy throb.

I kissed him with a desperation that grew by the second. I hadn't realized how deep my craving had grown in such a short time, but from the moment he burst into my house, Drake had been on my mind. And tonight, enjoying the concert with him, sharing the space, the energy—yeah, he'd stolen my attention.

It didn't hurt that he had the sort of muscles I wanted to trace with my tongue and wicked, bad-boy good looks.

He nipped at my lower lip, the zip of pain lighting my senses. My hips shifted on instinct, and my length brushed against the side of one of his thick thighs. Drake let out a low groan that reverberated against my mouth, a sinful sensation I wanted to revel in.

He pulled back at last, and breaths exploded between us.

"See? Trouble," he murmured. "I wasn't supposed to do that."

My heart thumped hard. I might miss cues a lot, but the fact he was Serena's brother was so obvious even I couldn't ignore it. "Well, if we're already making trouble, why not go out with a bang?"

He arched a brow, and I ground my cock against his thigh again, even the slight motion sending a shudder through me. His groan lit the air, low and delicious. His thick lashes fluttered, and then his serious, dark gaze locked in on me. He was going to turn me down. Tell me this was all a mistake.

My chest sank.

A wicked grin cracked his features, a canine poking out. "Last one to the pier's on their knees."

A thrill rushed me, as fierce and sudden as the rapids, and my smile rose unbidden.

"You're on."

Little did he know, I had every intention of letting him win.

Chapter Eight

Drake

I was a bad, bad man.

Sleeping with Serena's ex was a shit thing to do.

And yet, my blood pumped so hot through my veins, and my cock was so hard I couldn't stop myself. I hadn't experienced this sort of voltage during a kiss... well, ever. I raced at top speed across the beach, sand flinging up behind me. I'd drop to my knees in a heartbeat for him, but I'd been eyeing those plush lips all night, and the fantasies of having them wrapped around my length motivated me now.

I drank in the salt air, the crash of the waves, the slight chill of the night. My pulse thrummed as I soared over the sand, my heart crash-colliding all over the place. My vision shook with my erratic steps as I careened forward, the pier getting closer and closer. Spending the concert with August, every brush of skin, every glance in his direction, had amplified my growing desire for him. The man was radiance personified, the opposite of this velvet night.

The grains of sand stung around my ankles, but I only pushed myself harder, my calves burning with the resistance. The pier loomed, and the need that mounted inside me had reached a deafening roar. Tonight was a fantasy come true—meeting a guy at a punk show, connecting more than expected, and chasing that desire to completion.

I pushed off a little harder as I vaulted the rest of the way to the pier. My shoulder met the decrepit wood with a thud as I slammed into it. Under the shade of the pier, we'd have relative privacy, even though a thrill rippled up my spine at the idea of fucking around in public like this.

My breaths heaved from me as I looked to August approaching with a casual jog.

I arched an eyebrow. "Not competitive?"

He offered a slanted grin. "Maybe I just want to be on my knees."

Heat roared through me, and my gaze zeroed in on those lush lips of his. Ngh. My pulse was already rapid, and it didn't slow at all as he reached the pier. Any lingering questions that August was straight or bi had been answered by the kiss, and he broadcast his interest loud and clear. I shoved any temporary guilt aside. It's not like my sister met all the guys I hooked up with.

August's blond hair swept across his forehead, tousled from the run, and when he flashed me a grin, his white teeth gleamed against his tanned skin. He was stunning from head to toe. His lanky frame, the tattoos peeking past hems, and his bright, expressive eyes. Fuck, I wanted to kiss him again.

"C'mere," I said, crooking my finger. He strode right up to me, and all I had to do was lean in. We crashed together, his lips on mine, and I drank in the decadent sweetness. I wound my fingers through his silken strands, savoring the brush of his trimmed beard and how it contrasted with the softness of those lips. My cock strained against my jeans, but I sank into the kiss, lapping into August's hungry mouth. My whole body lit up like a landing strip from his touch, from our connection. I'd tangled with enough guys to understand this didn't happen with everyone.

When we pulled away, my shoulders heaved as I gasped for breath. August grinned again, his lips spit-slicked and pretty.

"I want more," he said, his gorgeous hazel eyes gleaming.

And then he sank to his knees in front of me. His fingers found the button of my jeans, and that was undone at a rapid pace. When he slid the zipper down, the sound was audible. I glanced around the beach, but we were hidden in the shadow of the pier, and few roamed the beach right now—definitely no one nearby. Excitement pumped through my veins, the exact sort I'd been yearning for.

August's legs were spread out, and he looked up at me. His eyes wide, gorgeous, and framed by thick lashes, lips parted in invitation.

"You're such a pretty picture on your knees," I murmured, reaching down to run my fingers along his chin. "You want my cock, beautiful?"

He swallowed hard, his Adam's apple bobbing. "Yeah. Desperately."

"Damn, aren't you perfect," I purred, reaching inside my boxer briefs. I shoved them and my jeans down to my thighs, and my cock sprang free. I ran my hand along my length. A shudder rolled through me at how good that felt. August licked his lips, his gaze zeroed in on my cock. He leaned up and lapped at the bead of precum on the tip. Bliss rushed through my veins from the mere contact. Everything around him was more loaded, my skin sensitized in his presence from the sheer electricity that percolated between us.

Chemistry like that couldn't be fabricated, no matter how hard you tried.

I wrapped my hand around the base of my cock and brushed the tip against his lower lip. "Come on, gorgeous. Suck me down."

August's eyes took on a feverish glaze as he leaned forward again. This time, his mouth encircled my tip, and the breath flew out of me. The sinful velvet heat, the light suction as he savored my cock, elevated me higher. He didn't just gulp me down and mechanically suck. No, August caressed the tip of his tongue against my slit, as if trying to urge more precum out, His lashes fluttered as he used his lips, the suction of his mouth, his tongue, to caress my head, to coax the pleasure out of me.

I tangled my fingers through his thick strands, wanting to let him explore but needing to ground myself. A soft moan escaped his lips, and fuck, that was so damn hot I forgot to breathe. He swallowed a few inches more, and the feeling of his hot, wet mouth wrapped around me knocked out any other thoughts from my mind.

My entire body coiled with tension from the intensity of the sensations rushing through me. He bobbed up and down on my cock, finding a slow and sinful rhythm that held me captive. Fuck, he felt so damn good. I hadn't realized how pent up I was, how much I held back until August ensnared my attention, rousing my libido back to life.

I tugged lightly on his hair, and he moaned again, the vibrations traveling my length. My balls were heavy as fuck, the need to come forming a bass snare beat. He took more and more of me into his mouth, swallowing me down his throat. My eyes rolled back in my head, and I let go of the loose grip I had around my base. Goddamn. August dipped his head in, bobbing with a fluid movement, which threatened to unmake me. His mouth was a silken heat, and the tight squeeze of his throat, the way he sucked me down with ease had me close.

I glanced at him, and his eyes shut in bliss suggested he was loving this as much as I was. Spit dribbled down his chin, dropping onto the sand below us, and he reached between his spread thighs. The hiss of a zipper sounded, and a second later, his arm began to pump.

God, that was so damn sexy.

The air sparked with the hint of danger, the reality that we were out in public, where anyone could stumble upon us. That fueled the heat brewing between us, threatening to scorch me from head to toe. The cool sand on my feet, the chilled salt breezes didn't do shit to tamp down the inferno raging inside me. My whole body coiled tight, ready to unleash.

I shifted my hips, fucking into August's mouth. He was full-out drooling, which was sexy as fuck, and he occasionally gagged a little when I thrust back in. He hadn't opened his eyes or stopped pumping at his own cock. I'd never gotten head this good before. I needed to come but never wanted this to end.

Goddamn. I tipped my head, raking my fingers through his silken strands. A long, low moan escaped me as I thrust into his throat. He spluttered around me, but the suction returned at once, the steady, velvet heat, the sinuous movements tempting enough to make me explode.

"You feel like sin," I groaned. "So fucking good, gorgeous."

August sucked a little harder at the praise, and I ran my fingers through his hair again, slowly pumping my cock inside all that decadent heat. His ass probably felt even better. My head swirled, and lust thumped at a steady beat inside me. Those ample, round cheeks, his long legs, messy hair. He'd look so stunning bent over and fucked.

I swallowed hard, my throat dry. Damn. Blistering desire rode me as I lost myself in the motions, thrusting in over and over. He returned the fervor, sucking my cock with desperation, as if he was close too. His arm shuttled faster, and he let out another moan around my length. My balls were so heavy, so full, I was going to burst. The tense thread in me pulled as taut as it could get, and the need for release had grown unbearable. Each bob of his head brought me closer, closer, closer.

August's gorgeous eyes fluttered open, and his moan was longer, louder, this time. The vibrations rolled right through me, and that was all it took.

"Fuck," I gasped as I came.

My balls drew up, and cum shot down his throat as my muscles tensed in pure ecstasy. My head tilted back, and I soared on the bliss that carried me higher and higher. My mind emptied, and I surrendered to the pleasure pouring into my veins. Everything relaxed as the endorphins took over, giving me the relief I'd been chasing.

August continued to suck on my cock, even as it began to deflate, and god, I never wanted to leave. I carded my fingers through his hair again and again as he sucked at my flaccid cock, as if he needed it in his mouth still. Lust shot through me at the idea of having his mouth on me as we drifted to sleep. Another fantasy to store in my spank bank.

I returned to reality, to the crash of the ocean near us, to the brisk salt breezes caressing our bare skin, to the shadowed silhouettes of the few walking the other side of the beach.

As much as I wanted to spend the night here, letting August suck my length, we needed to go.

Still, I carded my fingers through his hair a few minutes longer. He rested his cheek against the inside of my thigh as he continued to cockwarm me. I'd never had a guy do that before, and hell, I didn't realize how much I'd love it. If August was mine... Fuck, I'd fill his holes as often as humanly possible.

My chest squeezed tight with want. Right, that way lay madness.

Reality settled in a little more, cutting through the hazy satisfaction that lingered around both of us. I drew my cock from his mouth, even though he chased it the slightest bit. Damn. He was fucking perfect.

Still on his knees, he stared up at me. His lips were puffy, red, and spit-slicked. I dropped to the sand in front of him and claimed them at once. He tasted salty from my cum, but goddamn, the softness against my mouth was exactly what I needed right now. I licked into his mouth, delivering a searing kiss before pulling back.

"You came?" I asked, glancing at the puddle in the sand by his spent cock.

August swiped his thumb against the trail of drool down his chin. "Mmm, yes."

"Damn shame I didn't get to do the job," I murmured, my pulse thumping. He looked so fucking hot undone like this, his blond strands splayed over his forehead, his hazel eyes blown.

"Raincheck?" he asked.

No. I should say no.

"Name the time and place," came out of my mouth instead. I sucked in a breath. God, this guy had me so twisted up I couldn't think straight. I pushed up to a crouch and offered August a hand. He placed his callused palm in mine, and I gripped tight as I surged to a stand, bringing him along with me.

I let go of his hand, and I hated the loss of touch. I hadn't experienced these sparks around a guy in a damn long time. And it was effortless around him, the way he set me at ease just by his presence.

With a few deft motions, I tucked my cock away and zipped myself up. August was doing the same, and regret pulsed through me that I hadn't gotten a chance to see or touch his cock. The urge to explore him head to toe with my tongue and teeth hit with an undeniable ferocity. He was so damn pretty, and I could guarantee he had other tattoos hidden beneath his clothes, waiting to be explored.

"Definitely not how I expected the concert tonight to go," I teased. "Blown by a hottie by the pier."

August ran a hand through his hair. "Hottie?"

I let out a low whistle. "You're fucking gorgeous, yeah."

He dipped his head as if he were embarrassed. "So, what are we supposed to do now? High five or some shit? Ass slaps?"

I arched a brow. "Not usually a hookup sort of guy?"

August shook his head and teased that lower lip between his teeth. Impulse struck me, and I followed it as I leaned in and pressed my lips to his. He melted at once, and satisfaction trickled through me, the kind I hadn't even realized I'd been chasing. August was addictive. Everything about him—his soft noises, his warm, inviting body, his innate sweetness.

And he was the exact person I shouldn't be chasing. Yet I hadn't felt this spark with anyone in so long, and the more time we spent together, the stronger it flared.

When I pulled back, his breaths came out choppier.

"We could always do that," I teased, then took a step back. "Want to race back to the boardwalk?"

August shook his head. "After orgasms? I'm more of a mosey guy."

"Fine, we can mosey our way back," I said, bumping my shoulder with him, any chance to get the burst of electricity from touch.

We set off down the beach, boots in hand, drifting close to each other, as if our orbits were destined to collide.

Tomorrow, I could worry about the fact I'd slept with my sister's ex.

Chapter Nine

August

I hated that I was nervous to meet with my parents.

I'd always been comfortable with them, whether I dropped by the house randomly or called on a whim, but after they'd dropped their news and I'd ditched, things had been awkward. We'd texted a bit, but my parents were clearly giving me the space I'd asked for instead of Mom's usual daily puppy GIFs.

However, we had to acknowledge the elephant in the room. I wasn't sure why anyone invited an elephant into a room anyway. Terrible party guests.

I stepped up to the entrance of Fun-Guy, our local mushroom-themed sports bar, my nerves all a-jitter. It didn't help that I'd been checking and triple-checking my phone ever since the concert.

Three days had passed, and clearly, Drake hated me and never wanted to see me again because we'd barely talked.

While sucking him off under the pier had been hot as hell, I left with a lingering disappointment because I didn't want to be a one-off.

I wasn't cut out for hookups.

Especially because my parents were already breaking up with me. Which sounded a bit incestuous when I thought about it, but the feeling hit the same. I sucked in a sharp breath and walked into the bar.

The TVs blared with a basketball game in the background, and one of the usual bartenders stood behind the bar. I knew most folks in town, either from growing up here or because they'd gotten tattooed at the shop, and Hal, I'd tattooed. He had a mini reaper on his ankle.

The little dopamine hit surged again, the one that always did when I realized people were walking around and living their lives with little bits of my art on their skin.

"Auggie, we're over here," Mom called, snagging my attention. Her and Dad sat at the tables on the left, beside the window. My heart twisted, a combination of relief and sadness. I hadn't finished grappling with the bombshell they'd dropped. Just distracted myself.

Though, damn, what a distraction Drake had been.

I headed over to greet my folks and gave my mom a hug first, then my dad. The relief was clear in their eyes, and guilt bubbled up that I wasn't able to be more lax about their whole uproot and move down to Florida.

"Thanks for coming out to lunch," Dad said, his blond hair the same thickness as mine, just shorter and threaded with gray. His eyes crinkled at the edges. "You were right that we should've mentioned it to you when we started thinking about the idea."

I swallowed hard. Appreciation flared inside me. "I mean, it would've helped, so I wasn't blindsided."

"You could always come with us," Mom said, a burst of hope in her eyes. My stomach churned.

"Finding a tattoo job isn't easy." Plus, I'd been here my entire life. The idea of uprooting unsettled me as much as the idea of my parents moving.

"About that," Dad said. "We called around in Sarasota, and there's a shop currently looking for an established artist."

I wrinkled my nose. Established was variable. I couldn't bring my book with me, so I'd be starting from scratch with clientele. I did at least have the necessary experience. I hated that my brain even started entertaining this, but the sad puppy faces my parents were giving me made me want to agree on the spot, even if I was conflicted.

Guaranteed I'd get sad puppy faces from the crew at Alchemy Ink too.

Whatever I chose, someone would be upset, and I hated situations like this with my whole being.

"Don't know," I said. "My dating prospects wouldn't be great in Sarasota. Who would I date? Someone your age?"

Dad shook his head. "Please, no. We're old. But we looked into that too. Sarasota's got a huge gay scene."

"I'm bi, Dad," I responded.

"We're just saying if you want to keep your options open," Mom offered. "Plus, I thought bisexuals liked gay bars too."

I rolled my eyes, even though amusement filtered through me. "We're fans of all types of bars."

"We ordered your favorite burger, if that's okay," Mom said, tilting her head in the direction of the waitress who approached carrying a laden tray. "We even asked for extra pickles."

"Yeah, of course," I responded, even though I didn't think I'd be able to eat much right now. Not with the way my gut churned. "Thanks."

The waitress placed the plates in front of us. A BLT for Mom, a turkey sandwich for Dad, and the burger for me. All our usuals at a place we'd gone to for years, and yet the dynamic felt completely different.

"Do you mind if I take some time to think on things?" I asked, needing to cut the tension between us. Mom's constant glances and Dad's quiet were indicative that they were both waiting too.

"Of course, of course," Mom said, waving a hand back and forth. "We put the house on sale, so who knows how long it'll take to move."

The news socked me in the stomach. This was all rushing in faster than I could prepare for.

That urge to get up and bolt thrummed inside me again, but I couldn't abandon them in the middle of the restaurant.

I ate some fries instead.

I chewed intently on each fry, focusing on the salt distribution and not the fact that my parents wanted me to uproot my life and come with them. Or the fact that beyond my job, I didn't have many prospects here. Rory wasn't going to renew our lease—he'd be moving in with Wyatt when the time came—and I kept striking out left and right with boyfriends and girlfriends.

The door to Fun-Guy opened, and in strolled the man I hadn't seen or heard from over the past few days.

Drake Castillo.

He wore the firehouse tee, stretched too perfectly across his wide shoulders, his cargos framing those thick thighs, and my mouth watered on instinct. I hadn't forgotten the way he'd kissed me until I was delirious, or how damn good the thick weight of his cock felt. I'd fantasized about having that inside me as well, but he seemed to be done with me based on the few texts back.

"—and we'd be closer to Grandma and Grandpa," Mom continued, clearly in the middle of a conversation I hadn't realized we were having.

Awareness filtered through me of Drake in the room, even as I returned my focus to my folks. "Have you been discussing this with them?" I asked.

"They're one of the reasons," Mom said. "Grandma's not walking around well anymore. She's struggling, and I want to be able to help her and Grandpa."

More guilt poured right over me. I hadn't even known they were having a hard time. When I called Grandma last month, she'd been as much of a firecracker as ever. "All I heard was about the mushrooms she was growing that looked like dicks."

Dad snorted. Mom's mother had always been on the raunchier side, and we loved her for it.

"Hey, August?" Drake's voice snared my attention.

He stood a few feet away and waved. My mouth dried, and words evacuated my mouth. This close, I was reminded of every stolen moment from our time at the pier after the concert. The entire night had been unforgettable from beginning to end.

"Shit, I'm sorry for interrupting," he said as he scanned over my parents.

"Mind if I go say hi?" I asked my folks. Both of them got a glint in their eyes that I didn't like because the last thing I needed was them interfering right now. Especially when they were trying to get me to leave the area.

"Sure, we'll be here," Mom said, giving me a shooing motion.

I hopped out of the seat, far too eager to be away from all the conflicting thoughts with my folks. Drake had already started toward the bar, and I strode up beside him.

"Just got off a shift?" I asked, taking in the bags under his eyes and the slight slump of his shoulders.

"Another twenty-four. After the concert, I got launched into the thick of it at work, and apparently everyone and their mother was having a kitchen fire this week. You started a trend." Drake rifled his fingers through his hair and flashed me a grin.

My insides flip-flopped. God, he was dangerous for my heart.

The bartender swung by, and he ordered himself a beer and a burger for takeout before looking back at me. "You want?" I shook my head, since my food and drink remained back at the table with my folks. "Sorry for not responding much," he continued. "Didn't expect to run into you here, but I'm glad I did."

"Me too," I responded, the relief instantaneous. Maybe he hadn't gotten sick of me yet. "Thought the question about feet had been too much, but apparently not."

He snorted. "I mean, look, when I'm operating on zero sleep, I can't comprehend what I'd do with webbed feet. Can I get back to you on that?"

"Mm, don't know," I said, tapping a finger against my chin. "It's kind of pressing information if we keep talking."

His brows wrinkled in confusion.

"Like, are you the sort who'd try to do some underwater tricks or jerk yourself off with your webbed feet?"

"Is this a test? Like if I say the latter, then you're done with me?" he teased, a wicked arch to his brow that I liked a bit too much.

"Oh, I'd try the latter," I commented. "I don't like living with missed opportunities."

The bartender swung over with his beer, and Drake took a sip. The glossiness on his lower lip was far too sexy, and the urge to lean in and lick it surged strong. Fuck, how was he this damn hot and still talking to me?

"So, were you serious about being a concert buddy?" he asked.

"Do octopi have three hearts?" I responded, excitement bursting through me. Not that I was short on friends, but our night together had been replaying in my mind ever since it happened.

He blinked at me. "I have no idea. Do they?"

"Yeah," I said, scratching at my nape. "Weird facts are kind of my territory, mostly due to art research. I've had to do a lot of nautical sleeves."

"Is there anything you hate to tattoo?" he asked, settling in his seat. I cast a glance back at my folks, but they were deep in discussion over at the booth where I'd abandoned them.

"Script and lettering aren't my favorite, but it's normal territory with the job. Big pieces are where I thrive." I chewed on my lower lip. "But about the concert?"

"Ah, yeah." A slow, sexy grin rolled to his features, and damn, I couldn't quite look away from him. "I'm in charge of setting up a fundraiser for the fire company this year, and I want to do something different."

"What, the spaghetti dinners aren't drawing in crowds?" I teased. I'd seen the random flyers around town every once in a while, but that seemed like such an odd thing to show up to. Did someone just stand there with a bucket of spaghetti in marinara and shovel it onto plate after plate?

Drake barked a laugh. "Yeah, not lately. So, I was thinking of trying a small show, local talent. Draw in a crowd, bring some energy to the place."

"Oh, is this a local band?" I asked. I loved trying out small, unknown bands. Stumbling upon someone good was like finding a hidden treasure you wanted to share with everyone.

"Yeah, so I understand if you wouldn't be interested—"

"Nuh uh, not getting out of this," I said. "I'm definitely in."

"I haven't even mentioned when," he said, shaking his head. Still, I'd count the grin on his lips as a good sign. His fingers were inches away from mine, and the temptation to brush against his just to feel the jolt was ever-present. That sort of electricity was rare, and I craved it.

"Mm, I'll make it work around my schedule," I said with a shrug. Truth be told, I wanted to spend more time around him, any way I could. This close, his scent tickled my nose, some cedar cologne and the hint of smoke. It intoxicated me.

"This Friday?" he asked.

I wrinkled my nose. Friday, I worked at the shop until close. "Are they the headliner? If it's later, I'll be there." I wanted to ask was if he wanted to cash in on the rain check from the beach. Granted, while I sure as fuck wouldn't pass up on more orgasms, I found I just wanted to be around him. Clearly, a terrible sign for keeping things light and easy between us.

"Yeah, the show doesn't start until nine." He swigged another gulp of beer, and I enjoyed the bob of his Adam's apple. "We can hang after if you want." Drake's gaze snagged mine, and the heat there lit me up from the inside out. Tension percolated between us, thickening the air as neither of us looked away.

I swallowed hard. I could be dense, but I was pretty sure I picked up what he was implying. "Yeah," I managed, my throat dry. "I'd like that."

The bartender returned, slicing through the tension with knife-like precision. He dropped off the takeout Drake had ordered, already in its Styrofoam container and plastic bag.

Drake swallowed the last of his beer and placed the glass onto the counter. "All right. I'd better be out of here," he said, scooping up his takeout and rising to a stand. Part of me wanted to beg for a few more minutes, but my folks were waiting over at the booth for me, and I needed to return to them. "See you Friday?"

I nodded. "I'll be there."

His gaze zeroed in on my lips, and for a moment, I hoped he was going to dip in and claim them again.

Instead, he lifted a hand in a wave and stepped off. Disappointment thudded through me as I watched him head out of Fun-Guy. Both of my parents were blatantly staring at me—I could feel the looks boring into me—but I wasn't going to give them a morsel. Not when Drake's sudden appearance had muddled my thoughts. My parents' offer to move with them felt light-years away, even if it had only been brought up a bit ago.

I sucked in a deep breath and forced myself back to the table.

I didn't have to give an answer yet, so for now, I'd enjoy each moment I got with Drake.

If he followed my normal dating pattern, this wouldn't end up lasting anyway.

Chapter Ten

Drake

S pring Fires was a mix of punk and alt, a good blend of what I was looking for to headline the fire station fundraiser. Sure, a show might scare away some of the folks who normally attended the spaghetti dinners, but Chief had wanted me to shake things up a bit.

I ran my fingers through my hair for the thousandth time since I'd arrived at the venue. I'd only been here for half an hour, early enough that the first band was still setting up. A few counties over, the music hall here wasn't a huge drive but had good draw from the Main Line, despite being smaller. The lights were already dimmed, and I loitered by the bar with the beer I'd grabbed.

I wasn't nervous for the band, and I'd attended a dozen and one shows by my lonesome.

However, I'd invited my sister's ex to come here with me, and I also wanted to fuck him again something fierce.

Which was all sorts of wrong. I scrubbed at my face. Fuck, I needed to talk to Serena, at least get a vibe off her to see how attached she'd been. She wasn't languishing over the breakup or anything, but still. Sticking my dick in her ex pretty much broke the sibling code.

Yet August had been all I could think about for a week straight. The rapture in his gaze when he'd sucked my cock, the brightness in his features. The goofy way he rambled about the weirdest topics. His tousled blond hair, the tattoos decorating his lithe limbs. Yeah, the guy was a stunner, but I also felt insanely comfortable around him. Which was a rarity.

The first band, Dumpster Toilet, launched into thrash punk, the discordant sound echoing through the place. People were trickling in, some taking the seats lined around the perimeter, others flooding to the center floor to watch. The lights flashed on stage, and the music boomed, and I settled back against the wall in the spot I'd claimed.

The pressure to succeed in this fundraiser had started to creep in. Not that Mom or Dad made me feel like I had anything to prove, but both Serena and Blair were effortlessly impossible to live up to. Serena was a lawyer, and Blair was in her residency as a doctor. Cream of the crop careers. Meanwhile, I had leapt straight into being a firefighter, which, while solid, didn't have the same prestige. And the odd hours had scared many a guy away.

I didn't mind hooking up, but lately, I'd been craving something real. I hadn't realized how badly until I met August. He was so genuine with his responses and reactions, and I craved spending time with him in a way I hadn't around anyone for a long while.

Pure trouble.

Dumpster Toilet counted off, then launched into their next song, another erratic tune that I wasn't vibing with. The band name fit the music. Going to small shows like this was always fun though, because you ended up with stories regardless. I chugged a little more of my beer, finishing off the dregs. They had a good variety on tap, this one spicy and hoppy. I strode back to the bar and placed the glass on the counter.

"Drake?"

I whipped around to spot the exact person I'd been waiting for. August strode up to me, looking fine as fuck. His blond hair was tamed, and he wore a black tank top that exposed more of the tats along his arms and torso. The camo pants clung to his thighs, making me want to peel them off him. His hand was still raised in a wave, a bright smile on his face that lit his features. My pulse thrummed.

"Let me buy you a beer," I said as he approached. "I was planning on another anyway."

He shook his head. "When are you going to let me buy?"

I shrugged. "You're cute. Let me handle it."

August's lips twitched in a grin. "So cute's the stipulation for free drinks?"

"Well, and willing to weather these concerts with me." I wrinkled my nose as Dumpster Toilet hit a loud crescendo.

"Yeah, uh," he said, casting a quick glance at the stage. "They're enthusiastic at least."

A bark of a laugh escaped me. "That's one way of putting it."

The bartender circled around to us, and I ordered two beers before returning my attention to August. He stood close enough to me that I could reach out and touch him, and the urge to lean in and claim his lips roared inside me. It had killed me not getting to touch and taste him when we'd run into each other at Fun-Guy, but he'd been there with his parents. And we hadn't discussed anything.

Like the fact we'd met over my sister.

Who he'd dated.

I sucked in a sharp breath, trying not to notice the whiff of amber and antiseptic, an odd combination that was uniquely him. With him so close to me, all sense flew out the window, and when the bartender swung back with our drinks, I stepped a little nearer to hand him his, making sure our fingers brushed. A zing rippled through me. His breath puffed against me, his eyes widening, and I bit my lower lip, forcing myself back.

Damn, I wanted to kiss him again.

"We are Dumpster Toilet," the lead singer called out. "Thank you, and good night!"

A ripple of claps rang out, as well as a few hoots. August and I shared a glance and smirked. God, it was fucking fun being here with him.

The band started to move their equipment, which meant Spring Fires should be next. I placed my hand on August's shoulder and tipped my head in the direction of the wall, so we could grab a closer spot. Problem was, once I touched him, I didn't want to stop. He looked up at me with those fuck-me eyes and lush lips, and goddamn. He licked his lips, and I was about to combust.

The need rose high in me, and I threw hesitation out the window.

I grabbed August by the shirt and tugged him forward as I backed up against the wall. His chest crashed against mine, and he opened his mouth, the question clear in his eyes.

I answered him with a kiss.

He melted against me like he belonged there, his palm resting on my chest. I drove my tongue into his mouth, deepening the kiss, savoring the spicy, crisp taste of the beer we'd drunk. My head spun from the sheer force of kissing him, the chemistry between us undeniable. I didn't have a hard time getting along with people, but rarely was the connection this effortless. Being around him was like soaking in the rays of the summer sun.

My cock woke up at our proximity, at the way his chest, his hips, pressed against mine. His body was hard and warm and begging to be explored thoroughly. My pulse sped at the thought of getting to take him apart with my tongue, my teeth. When had I experienced an intense fixation like this before? Not in a damn long while, that was for sure.

I savored his lips against mine, the way awareness crackled through me. He moaned, the vibration humming against my mouth. Fuuuck. I wanted to bury my cock inside him. His length nudged against my thigh, signaling I wasn't the only one affected.

The whine of the microphone split the air. "You all ready to start some fires?"

Fire? I yanked back from August, my adrenaline kicking in before my gaze landed on the band that had arrived on the stage while we'd been making out.

Spring Fires.

My fucking god. I let out a groan and scrubbed my face.

"Look, it's your calling card, fire boy." August snorted, his eyes crinkling with amusement. "Were you ready to dash off for an extinguisher?"

"Shut up," I muttered, the sound muffled with my palms on my face. Clearly, I'd been working as a firefighter for too long. But seriously, shouting fire in a venue wasn't the smartest plan.

My brain whirred. Wait, maybe we could work that into a bit.

If I could even convince them to do the fundraiser show.

The first song kicked off, fast-paced and fun. I found my foot tapping instinctively. I'd checked out their music online ahead of time, and they had a pretty wide range between punk and alt rock. Plus, they were ridiculously talented.

August craned forward. "Is that Ethan?"

"What?" I asked, scanning the stage. The band had a lot of energy, everyone in motion, and the crowd reacted in turn. It was such a dynamic shift between the last act and this one, and I couldn't help but notice.

"The vocalist," August said. "I'm pretty sure that's Ethan."

"That an ex?" I asked. The guy singing was the quintessential scene guy—black gauges, dark hair, guyliner. Definitely attractive, but he didn't hold a candle to August. No one had captured my attention like him in a long, long while.

"Nah, a client," he said, his elbow brushing against mine. The thrill that rippled through me from the mere touch was incendiary. All too easily I could imagine finding a dark corner, a bathroom stall, and crowding him up against it, fucking him until he was babbling. Except something about our last encounter had struck a spark within me, and this fantasy had burned through my brain until it was all I could think about.

And if he came home with me tonight, we'd have the chance to fulfill it.

His words broke through the haze of lust that descended. "Wait, a client of yours? Like you could get me in contact with him?" I asked, then realized how that sounded. "Unless that crosses some lines."

August shook his head, his blond strands moving with the motion. "Nah, he's always asking about gigs. These guys would be a great fit for your fundraiser."

My heart thumped hard. There was an ease to August that I craved, like the languid waves rolling to the shore, so different from the adrenaline I normally chased. He lured me in, like a tether to stop a free fall, and I couldn't help but text him, make plans, touch him, kiss him. Fuck.

Standing next to him and not having my hands all over him was driving me insane. I wanted to touch him constantly, just to get the feedback loop of electricity that existed between us.

"Yeah, if we could book these guys, I could guaranteed bring in some money to fix up the kitchen."

August wrinkled his nose. "I think he's in my book tomorrow. Want me to ask?"

I swallowed hard, trying to tamp down my excitement. Everything about August ticked my boxes—his goofy sense of humor, his insane talent, his calm energy. Two concerts in and we'd wandered far outside of hookup territory.

And I didn't hate it, even though I should.

"Shit, if you don't mind," I said, clutching my nape. The lights flashed as Spring Fires ended their first song, and I let out a holler in appreciation. The crowd lit up with shouts and applause, but the band didn't even hesitate before launching into their next song.

I inched closer to him, so our shoulders bumped.

August glanced my way, and his breath hitched. Fuck. The urge to kiss him again rose something fierce, but I'd come here to check this band out, not to make out with a hottie.

"What are you doing after the show?" I asked, hedging my bets.

August's eyes grew a little more intense. "I'm free."

"Want to come over?" I asked. The tension percolated in the air between us, thick and pervasive. He licked his lips, the light gloss there entrancing.

"Only if I can crash at yours," he said, an impish grin on his lips.

I couldn't help the smile that rolled to my lips. "Like I'd let you out of my bed."

Chapter Eleven

August

I rolled up in front of Drake's house, a pale colonial with a dark roof. It cut a pretty figure on the street, even this late at night. My pulse thrummed, and not from the excellent show I'd just seen. Ethan had been talking about his band for a while now, and I'd always meant to get out to see them. Just so happened I got to on this not-date.

And of course Drake was ridiculously hot, kissed me until I was delirious, and exuded this competency and spark of danger that I was addicted to.

Not a great recipe for casual hookup.

But I couldn't ask for more when I'd started looking at rentals in Florida. Which felt wrong, but what could I do? Say no to my folks? They'd looked so sad.

I pressed my forehead to the steering wheel and sucked in a deep breath to compose myself. Then I left the car, locked it, and headed down the front pathway to Drake's front door.

I'd barely lifted my knuckles to knock when the door swung open.

I'd just seen him back at the music hall, but the sight of him knocked the breath from my lungs. His dark hair was swept to the side, and his jeans clung to those muscled thighs like SecondSkin. The fantasies of him fucking me, of him staying inside me through the night, had roared to life and refused to leave. Fuck, part of me was dying to let him in bare, even though we'd need to talk beforehand.

"Come on in," he said, turning on his heel and heading farther into his place.

I followed, bringing the door shut behind me. The walls weren't decorated with much, all eggshell white like he'd never painted after moving in. Honestly, it surprised me. With how full of life he was, how much he lived, I expected his place to explode with color. The bare walls made my fingers itch, made me want to paint.

"Going to offer me a drink or your cock?" I asked as we wandered past the foyer and by the stairs.

Drake let out a bark of a laugh. "Depends on what you'd prefer to drink."

"Your cum, clearly," I responded, warmth rousing in my chest. The way his eyes scorched as he scanned me over left me a little breathless. I didn't know why I'd bothered with clothes if he was going to eye-fuck me that hard.

"I've been fantasizing about this ass," he said, taking another step toward me until there were mere inches between us. He reached around and grabbed my ass hard. My cock woke to life at once.

"Oh yeah?" I asked, arching a brow. "What do you want to do to it?"

He kept his firm grip on my ass as he stared down at me, mere inches between our bodies, the tension excruciating. "I want to bend you over and pry your cheeks open, then rim you until you're in tears. Then I want to sink inside you and fuck you until you forget your name."

"Ngh, yes," I moaned, the images flashing through me fast and furious.

"And then I want to stay inside that pretty little hole for as long as possible, teasing and toying with your cock while you wait to come," he said, his voice pure velvet and gravel.

Flames roared through me. It was like he'd plucked straight into my head and pulled out the secret desires I harbored. "Do you need me to beg? Because I'll fucking beg."

"No need, baby," he murmured as he let go of the grip on my ass. His palm slid against mine, and he gave my hand a tug. "Follow me."

He led me up the staircase, and I couldn't help but fixate on the cocky saunter, his muscular ass on full display in those Levis. I chewed on my lower lip until I tasted blood. Damn, he was five-alarm hot, and I still couldn't believe we were hooking up. Even though he seemed like the cool guy, the bad boy, never once had he made me feel dumb or too much for the excessive amounts I texted him and the random questions that popped into my head.

And after having his thick, heavy cock in my mouth the other night, I'd been dying to get him inside me.

"Bedroom's here," he said as he guided us to the left and in through the open door. The hallway was equally undecorated, which struck me as odd.

"Spartan lifestyle?" I asked, giving a glance to the walls.

"More like terrible taste and no drive. Maybe if it wasn't just me here..." he trailed off and shook his head, like he was clearing an

Etch-A-Sketch. "Come on. Going to decorate my house or get in my bed?"

"The latter," I said, rushing past him in the room. I didn't hesitate, just leapt for his bed, arms out like I was a flying squirrel or some shit. I landed face-first into the mattress with a whumph.

The lights flickered on, and I flipped over onto my back. Drake stood by the doorframe, his arms crossed, which only placed his veiny forearms on display. His eyes twinkled with amusement.

"You're a little overdressed for bed," he said, his voice husky.

The tension in the room heightened, and the air thickened between us.

"Oh, no-clothes policy?" I teased, playing with the button of my jeans.

"I need you stripped down and on my sheets." Drake prowled over until he stood before me. The sight of him looming over got me hotter, my cock rigid. Damn, he was a fantasy come to life.

"Don't know," I said, stretching to fold my hands behind my head. "I'm pretty comfortable."

He shook his head, a grin rising to his lips and a feral look in his eyes. Goddamn. I'd been with partners who were fire in the sheets, but no one had looked at me with singular focus, the sort of intensity that burnt down buildings.

Drake reached for the hem of my shirt and forced it up, exposing my abs. He traced his fingertips along the surface, and the touch ignited all the desire that bubbled inside me. When he gave the tug, I pushed up and helped him yank my shirt up and over my head, my arms. Then he snapped the button on my jeans, and I shrugged those down too, bringing my boxer briefs along with them. I kicked off my shoes and then extricated myself from my pants the rest of the way before peeling my socks off. All too fast, I was stripped down on Drake's bed, exposed to him entirely.

Anticipation thudded through me as he prowled onto the bed, bracketing me with his body, his palms pressing into the mattress on either side of me. Mere inches separated us, and I ached to close it. Except the tension that spread between us held a powder keg note, as if at any moment we'd detonate. My cock strained, pre-cum pooling at the tip. Drake planked overtop me, his hot breath puffing against my face.

"I'm going to taste every inch of you," he said, the heat in his tone drifting over me like a caress. "Going to map your body with my teeth, my tongue, my mouth."

"Yes, please," I gasped, far breathier than intended. His dark eyes were magnetic, a wildness to them, to the arch of his brows that held me enraptured. God, I needed him inside me. Instead, Drake leaned in and pressed a kiss along the side of my neck. He nipped at the corded muscle there, and a shiver raced through me. He then lowered to lick along my collarbones, savoring each motion rather than rushing. I'd never had a partner take me apart like this, deliver such attention to detail.

I'd never felt so exposed, so seen.

I fucking adored it.

Drake continued lower, and the tip of his tongue circled my nipple. A moan escaped me—I was a slut for nipple play—and he took one bud into his mouth and sucked.

"Oh fuck!" My hips lifted off the bed, my stiff cock brushing against his stomach. He moved to the other one to suck that into his mouth too, and I fisted the sheets on either side of me. Drake seemed to realize what a spot it was for me, because he launched into a relentless attack with sucks and nips. Moans poured out of me, and my cock leaked like a faucet.

"God, the sounds you make are gorgeous," Drake said, reaching between us to brush his thumb over the tip of my cock. "And you're making such a sticky mess of yourself."

Heat rushed through my body, fast and fierce. His mouth was filthy, and I fucking loved it.

Drake dragged his tongue down my stomach, the movement slow and sinuous. My breaths came out choppy, sweat beading on my forehead. Fuck, I was burning up from the inside out.

"Fuck me," I begged.

Drake looked up, and the wicked arch of his eyebrow said every-thing. "I'm not done with you yet, baby."

The endearment caused more warmth to bloom inside me. The possessive way he said it and the intensity in his gaze made me hope a little too hard that I wasn't just a hookup for him. But tonight I'd simply enjoy whatever he had in store for me.

Drake nipped down my hipbones, my cock straining, begging for attention. The head was almost purple it was so needy. As much as I wanted to reach down and give it a stroke, it felt even better surren-dering to him. Letting him take control.

"You're so good for me," he murmured, pressing kisses along my hips. "So pliant, so sweet."

A shameful whimper escaped my lips, and my whole body flushed.

"Pretty boy likes some praise?" he asked before pressing another kiss, right on a sensitive spot. My hips bucked up again.

"Yes," I gasped out, clutching the sheets harder to keep from reach-ing for myself. "Oh god, yes."

"Well, you keep being so, so good, and I'll have plenty for you," he said. His breath puffed against my cock, and I groaned. My balls throbbed, the need to unload excruciating. I needed him to touch, to lick, fuck, anything.

Instead, Drake situated himself between my legs, spread them wide, and brushed his thumb across my hole.

"Fuuuck," I moaned.

"Mmm, see?" he teased. "So good. And this pretty hole is begging for attention."

Where the hell did he even come from? I'd never had sex with anyone who dirty talked like him, and goddamn, how had I been living without this? Before I could ask, Drake lowered his head. His tongue brushed against my hole, and the shockwave of sensation rushed through me.

"Oh, oh god," I gasped. He dipped his head again and his tongue painted a filthy stripe from my taint to my hole. Any remaining coherency flew out the window. Drake ate me out like I was his last meal, and the keening noises that emerged from my mouth were brand new. No one had ever taken me apart like this before, but hell, I liked it far too much.

He licked and sucked at my hole, then he thrust his tongue inside. I tilted my head back, surrendering to the sensations that amped up with each pass of his mouth. My entire focus was on him, his hands on my body, his mouth making me unravel. My thighs began to tremble from how good his attention felt, and my cock gushed more pre-cum.

When he pulled back, he gave my ass a hard squeeze and flashed me a cocky grin. His lips glistened with spit from the way he'd lapped at me. "Look at all this gorgeous ink," he murmured, brushing his fingertips along my ribs where I'd gotten a particularly painful lighthouse tattoo. "You're a work of art."

Ngh. If he kept talking to me like this, I was liable to combust. I squirmed on the mattress and spread my legs a little wider.

Drake tapped his fingers at my hole. "And this... damn. I could happily live between your legs."

The moan that erupted from me was full-throated, and heat roared through me. "Yes, yes, yes."

His grin was sinful, the slightest hint of teeth showing, and the glitter in his dark eyes set my veins on fire. "I'm negative, but I'll grab protection," he said. I hadn't gotten tested since I'd been with Serena, but I had the feeling bringing that up right now would splash cold water over things. And if I didn't get him inside me, I would scream. So, I chewed on my lower lip instead and watched as he tugged off his shirt, then dropped his briefs and pants in one go, kicking the pile of clothes and boots to the side.

Stripped down, Drake Castillo was fucking magnificent.

His dark hair was splayed messily across his forehead, and his tan skin had an even glow to it I found alluring. The tattoos he had were good, a thigh one of ravens, a small flame symbol on his hip, close to his groin. I'm sure he hid more, and I wanted to explore all of him. But right now, I wanted him inside me more than anything. A dark trail of hair led to his firm length, which was veiny and curved slightly to the left. His muscled arms and legs promised the strength to deliver right now. Drake ripped open a rubber and slid it on, then slathered his cock in lube.

And damn, what a cock it was. My mouth watered at the sight of his thickness, the knowledge he'd be sliding right inside me any minute now. Goddamn.

"Hell, you look so good like that," he murmured as he stepped between my legs. "Spread open for me, waiting for my cock. You're going to feel so damn amazing."

"I need you," I gasped, the delay agonizing. My balls were so heavy from the time he'd spent tasting every inch of me, and fuck, I just wanted to feel him splitting me open. Railing me until I was delirious.

His tip nudged against my hole as he gripped my thighs tight, taking control. "How long as it been?" he asked.

"Since I've gotten fucked or since I've used a toy?" I asked. I'd always been a slut for being penetrated. When I was with guys, I bottomed, and when I was with girls, I'd had some success in getting them to peg me. "The latter was the other night. And I like a big toy."

Drake swore as he pushed down on his length. "You're a walking wet dream. You know that, right?" He nudged the tip of his cock against my hole, and I tried to spear myself on it. He gave my thighs a tight squeeze. "Patience. I've got this."

I hadn't realized how much competency was a turn-on, but damn, every time he took control with ease, my pulse quickened. Slowly, he began to push inside me, driving me wild. The smirk on his lips was just as infuriating as it was sexy.

"Please," I begged, shifting my hips to try to take more of him inside me.

He squeezed my thighs again. "Well, since you asked so nicely..." Drake maintained eye contact with me the entire time as he thrust the rest of the way in with one stroke.

The thickness was enough for my breath to hitch, a slight burn I'd been craving. Fuuuuck. The fullness, how he stretched me out, the length... it was everything I needed. His fingertips dug into my thighs, and he swore.

"Damn, you're so tight, baby," he murmured. "Don't know which I need more, your mouth or your hole."

"You can have both, any time you want," I panted. "Just move."

"Dangerous offer," he said, his eyes glinting.

I meant it. More than he realized. I usually held back from sharing how much of a cockslut I was with partners. It hadn't gone well in the past, but, damn, the fantasies parading through my mind had him spilling inside me, parked in my hole as long as humanly possible. Had my mouth wrapped around him, sucking him to sleep.

Drake drew back, and the sudden motion knocked the breath from me. When he thrust in, his cock grazed my prostate, and sparks flared. I cried out at the same time he let out a groan.

"So. Damn. Good." He punctuated each word with a thrust, and all I could do was hold on for the ride. I gripped the sheets tighter on either side as I rolled my hips to meet him every time he fucked into me.

"Ohhhh." The moan escaped me long and loud as he drove into me in earnest, a concentration in his knitted brow that was beyond hot. I surrendered to sheer sensation, to the steadfast thrust of his hips to the zing of pleasure whenever he brushed against my prostate. He was large enough to command my full attention, his length stretching me out in the way I craved but rarely found outside of my toys.

"Damn, this hole is silk," he murmured. "You're so hot and tight, baby. I don't ever want to leave. I could pump load after load in here until you were dripping."

I incinerated. Fuck, had he reached right into my head and plucked out my fantasies? My legs trembled as he fucked me with a deliberateness that got me hot. He'd draw back far enough that a plea almost rose in my throat but then slide in slow and easy, like he savored the ride. Fireworks burst behind my eyes again, each slam of his cock nailing my prostate. The moans that escaped me were loud enough to tremble through the room.

"God, I could fuck you for the rest of the night," he rasped. "Just to feel the clasp of your hole around me."

Another whimper escaped me. I wanted that so bad, even if I didn't know if I could take it. I'd never slept with someone who tapped into my desires this easily, and goddamn, the difference was revolutionary.

He continued to thrust in at an even tempo, and the heat roared through me to the point sweat beaded on my skin. My breaths came out choppy, mingling with the gasps and moans that continued to erupt from me. He had a rhythm I adored, not the jackhammer speed to nut style but a deliberate pace, like he was determined to enjoy every last second of this.

His breaths grew faster, sharper, and his thick brows drew together, an intensity to his features that made him even hotter. His grip on my thighs was tight, and each time our skin slammed together, sparklers flared inside of me. My balls grew heavier and heavier, my cock desperate for touch

I reached out for it, but Drake batted my hand away. "That's my job," he said, flashing me a cocky grin. "I've got a plan."

Damn if that wasn't the hottest thing to hear. I resumed grabbing the sheets like my life depended on it as he drove his cock into me again and again. Drake pumped into me faster, his breaths quickening in turn.

"Fuck, I'm going to come." His thighs tensed, his head tilted back, exposing his gorgeous Adam's apple, and his cock throbbed as he emptied inside me. His long, low groan split the air, sexy as fuck, and his lashes fluttered. He squeezed my thighs tight enough to bruise as he came, and the sensation kept me grounded in the moment.

Drake sucked in a sharp breath. "Let's shift," he murmured as he moved my leg to one side and then twisting until he was lying on the bed. His cock hadn't deflated yet, but curiosity rippled through me at what he had planned. Curiosity and a little bit of desperation. Drake arranged us so he was spooning my back, his cock still buried inside my hole, even though the rubber kept me from feeling the leak of his cum.

"Good," Drake said as he wrapped his palm around my cock. "Now I can take my time with you while you warm my cock."

Oh fuck. My cock leaked in response, and I didn't bite back my whimper. "How…"

"You're pretty easy to read, August," he murmured, pressing his lips against my sweaty nape. He then licked and bit at it all while he slowly stroked at my length. His cock had started to deflate, but he didn't make any moves to pull out, and I loved that more than I could express. Something about being filled flipped my switches in the best way, and I hadn't even needed to voice those wants—Drake had figured them out and made it happen.

With him pressed up against me like this, our sweaty bodies plastered together, I couldn't help but drink in the scent of sweat and cedar that surrounded me. A shiver rolled through my whole body. He continued to stroke my cock with the same languid pace that he fucked, but all too fast, my balls began to draw up.

"Oh—"

Drake let go.

The impending release receded, and I let out a groan. "Why?"

"Because you're going to keep my cock nice and cozy for a while, and I'm going to play with your cock the whole time," Drake teased.

"You're going to kill me," I muttered.

"I think you'll survive," he said as he wrapped his callused palm around my length again. "In fact, I think you even like it."

"Monster," I said, fucking into his fist a little more. Except that shifted his deflated cock inside me, and a moan escaped me as I settled. He sank his teeth into my shoulder, casually biting and sucking at the skin, his mouth the most talented I'd ever experienced. Every simple motion amplified my desire.

"I'm only a monster if you don't enjoy it," he teased, as he ran his palm up and down my cock. "But it seems to me like you're enjoying yourself."

I bit down on my lip until I tasted blood. My balls ached something fierce, the need to come rising in me stronger by the second. He wasn't wrong. I loved that he toyed with me while his cock remained buried inside me. As if we did this any night of the week, him leisurely keeping his cock warm in me while he played with my body like he owned it. I lit up in flames for the thousandth time since we'd gotten to his room, but thankfully he was the perfect person to handle them. God, I didn't want this to end.

Having a partner who I connected with this easily—damn, that was the dream.

Drake nipped at my earlobe, sending a shiver through me, and he quickened the way he jerked me off. All too fast, my breaths quickened, and droplets of sweat beaded on my forehead, a few trickling down.

"Oh god, oh god," I gasped, the urge to come barreling up again.

Drake let go.

"Fuckingfuckyou," I groaned, tipping my head back. His muscular frame pressed up against me, the skin-to-skin connection lighting me up inside. Almost as much as his flaccid cock still resting inside my hole. The only way it'd be better was if he was bare.

Drake chuckled, his chest rumbling with the sound. "Pretty sure you'd prefer it the other way around. Though, I guess you're verse?"

"Pretty sure I'd rather be coming than conversing," I gasped.

He wrapped his hand around my cock again, continuing the leisurely stroke along my cock. It was so sensitive at this point I could scream, my balls primed and ready for release. Even though he pulled back when I was close to coming, each time brought me closer and closer to the edge. And already, I could feel the familiar tension brewing inside me, growing stronger with every shift of his warm palm.

"Had enough, baby?" he teased, amusement in his voice.

"Please let me come," I begged, not even caring how shameless I sounded.

"Since you asked so prettily," he murmured, brushing his lips against my nape again in a casual kiss. The gentle sensation contrasted with the way he quickened shuttling his hand up and down my length. I swooned. The filthiness mixed with tenderness was everything I'd ever wanted in a partner.

Drake's teeth grazed against my skin, and a keening noise escaped me. I was trapped between his body, his cock still lodged inside me, and his hand moving along my cock at a rapid pace. I loved it, more than I thought I would. The feel of his palm against my sensitive cock brought me closer and closer to the edge. My breaths came out choppy and fast, sweat breaking out on my thighs. Fuck.

My balls ached so badly I wanted to scream, and each stroke had me nearing explosion.

"Please," I gasped. "Please."

"So good," he murmured, his voice velvet. "Come for me."

The orgasm slammed into me hard enough that my vision shuddered. I shouted long and loud as my balls drew up and a thick and heavy load shot from my cock. It splattered onto the sheets in front of me, and my body tensed from the sheer force of the release. I coasted on pleasure as fireworks exploded behind my eyes, commanding my sole attention.

Damn, I didn't want to leave this cocoon of bliss. With Drake pressed up behind me, his arms wrapped around my body, his cock buried in me, I could float here forever. If he wanted to spend the entire night in me, I wouldn't complain.

"Damn," Drake said. "Keep squeezing my cock like that and it's liable to wake up again."

I snorted and reached up to wipe the sweaty strands plastered to my forehead. "Mine's spent. You edged me enough that I'm dead. Deceased."

"And dramatic too, apparently," he said.

I wrinkled my nose. "I fucked up your sheets. Sorry."

"Pretty sure that's what washing machines are for," he said. "Plus, damn. That wasn't a small amount. Storing up for a while?"

I toyed with my lower lip between my teeth. The truth was, no one had ever wrung an orgasm from me like that. The sheer amount of time and attention he'd spent on my body, how he'd tapped into my deepest fantasies—Drake was perfect.

And we were in the worst timeline for more. Him being my ex's brother. Me considering a move down South.

"You just fucked me that good," I responded, forcing myself to stay in the moment.

"As much as I'd love to stay in you all night, the rubber makes that hard," he said. "But I'll stay a little longer, okay?"

"God, yes."

My heart thumped harder, and I settled against the mattress. I wanted something like this more than I wanted my next breath. A partner to cozy up with at the end of a day, someone to coast along life with and navigate the hurdles when they arose.

But those dreams felt a little too bright, a little too hot to touch with all the complicating factors.

Tonight, I'd just bask in this bliss I'd found with him.

Chapter Twelve

Drake

Normally, I was ambivalent about family gatherings. It was always good to see everyone, though half the time I showed up exhausted. My job didn't lend itself to normal shifts, though neither did my sisters', yet they still managed to be functional. Tonight, though? Tonight I was worried.

I pulled up to Byrne's Tavern, a more upscale place on the outside of town. Blair wanted quality food for her birthday, so that was where we were going, even though I'd have been just as satisfied with a cheesesteak from Sal's.

I hadn't seen Serena since I'd swung by her place to grab the stuff to drop off at August's.

And now, I'd fucked her ex not once but twice.

Even worse? I wanted to do it again. And again and again. August had crashed in my bed that night, and if we both hadn't needed to get to work, I would've asked him to stay the rest of the day. Being around him was addictive. I hadn't been able to enjoy myself with a guy on an intimate level like that in so damn long. With hookups, it had always been out before the sheets cooled, and boyfriends hadn't lasted long. Too often, my odd schedule came into conflict with theirs, or our interests didn't converge enough, and we ended up drifting apart.

I'd had more fizzled out relationships than I could count, which made me feel like I was either uninteresting or inaccessible.

Maybe both.

I shut off the engine and got out of my car, the brisk air skating across my skin. Mom had messaged that they were inside, so I didn't hesitate and strode up to the main door. Once I stepped inside, the scent of cedar surrounded me, the lighting dim for ambiance. This place was upscale rustic, the farmer chic look people were crazy for nowadays, but I liked it well enough. Better than the white tablecloth places Serena made us trot out to.

I scanned the room, the polished pine tables already filling up, and caught my parents and sisters sitting in the far back. They all looked like they fit right in, Serena in her black pantsuit, Blair in a cream blouse and skirt, prim and neat accessories. I'd worn a nice pair of Levi's and a plaid button-down, but I lacked in the classy clothes department. Kind of came with the territory when you grew up a punk and ended up a fireman. Even Mom and Dad had the business professional attire down, and altogether, I felt out of place. Like everyone else was an adult and I just cosplayed.

"Hey," I said, nearing the table.

Mom got up from the seat and squeezed me into a hug. "Put out any fires recently?"

I snorted, so used to her regular opening question that it was hard to hold back the eye roll. Still, I gave her a tight hug, her floral perfume a punch of familiarity. Dad hopped up too and hugged me next, then Serena and Blair followed suit, both of them crowding me at once. Comfort flowed through me at being around my family, despite the fancy setting.

Even though I was sleeping with Serena's ex.

Guilt prickled through me as I took the open seat they'd left for me. "What were you all talking about?"

"Crazy day at the hospital," Blair sighed. "You'd think it was a full moon."

"That's when all the arsonists come out," I said, as I skimmed over the menu. "It's like they find it inspirational or some shit." My nose wrinkled at the prices. I made enough to comfortably live on, but a firefighter's salary wasn't anywhere near what my sisters were bringing in.

"Criminals tend to operate year-round," Serena said. "Full moon or no."

"Mmk, Miss Fancy Prosecutor," I said, landing on an overpriced burger. I much preferred the type I'd had at Red Square Diner not so long ago. With August. Ugh, I couldn't stop thinking about him.

"Did you have fun at the show?" Serena asked, and I straightened in my seat.

"What do you mean?" The words came out a little sharper than intended.

"You know, the show I gave you a ticket for? You went, right?" she asked, her brows lifting.

Heat rushed to my cheeks. Right, the one where August had blown me by the pier. That one.

"Yeah, it was great. Solid openers, and the band is amazing," I said, hoping my eagle-eyed sister couldn't suss out my guilt. Even though that was what she did for a living.

"August has the same taste in music as you, so I figured you'd be better suited to go." She gave me a careful scan over, like she was piecing together something I hid. Last thing I needed was an interrogation at the table.

"Mom, did you get the wart on your foot looked at?" I asked in a rush.

Mom passed me a sour look, her nose wrinkling. "I don't think everyone in the restaurant wants to hear about that."

Serena's gaze burned into me from across the table, and sweat prickled on my forehead. How was I going to survive family events? My sister was one of the best people at extracting the truth, and she was a manipulative motherfucker. Either I had to stop sleeping with August, or I had to come out with the truth.

And right now, I didn't want to do either.

The server swung over to my relief, and we placed our orders.

"What's new at the firehouse?" Blair asked.

I squeezed my nape. Sure, I had the fundraiser I was attempting to put together, but without the band booked, I didn't want to bring anything up. If my idea flopped, I didn't want my family to witness it—they'd seen enough of my second-rate attempts over the years. "Uh, Hannigan got stabbed in the ass with his Halligan, which is something he's never going to live down."

Dad snorted. "Maybe not dinner conversation, but that's hilarious."

Right. I was so used to hanging around the firehouse where no one gave a shit about manners that this sort of thing was excruciating.

I'd dated a few guys who worked corporate, and they'd had similar problems with me.

August, on the other hand, was easy as hell to be around. Maybe because we both worked unconventional jobs, but damn, I never felt judged by him. Never felt less than. Sure, having overachiever sisters meant I got in my head a lot, but he was a breath of fresh air I hadn't realized I'd needed this badly.

"How are you feeling in your wizened age?" I teased Blair, who rolled her eyes.

"Far too single," she muttered. "I thought Kyle would be the one, but he ended up being another jerk." We'd all been relieved when that crashed and burned. Kyle had been around for two years. They'd met in med school, and he'd been insufferable. I'd never met anyone who complained so much in my life.

"Psh, not me," Serena said. "I'm loving being single and free again."

"Not missing your ex?" Hearing her words were reassuring, but I grasped for anything extra to assuage my guilt.

Serena blinked. "August? God, we were barely dating. He's an adorable guy, but I was looking for a fling, not a relationship. And he's got relationship written all over him."

I swallowed hard, my throat tight. I was well aware of that. What was worse was the more time I spent around him, the more I craved having him in my life regularly. But this wasn't the same as getting a hand-me-down toy from Serena when we were kids. Boyfriends weren't in the acceptable hand-me-down category.

"Will any of you be giving me grandchildren?" Dad sighed, even though a twinkle was in his eyes. Out of our parents, Dad was the baby crazy one. Mom was more interested in the next article in Science Journal. As a microbiologist, she was constantly studying up on new things.

"Count me out," I said. "I can't even find a guy willing to weather my schedule enough to settle down."

"I don't know what's wrong with the guys you're dating," Blair said. "My residency schedule is shit, but worthwhile people will stick around."

"Oh, like Kyle?" Serena teased while Blair rolled her eyes.

I forced a smile, but my chest sank. Blair hadn't meant an insult, but her comment cracked right through the flimsy shield I'd been wielding to cover why my relationships never panned out.

Work. I always blamed work.

Truth was, I wasn't worth staying for. Too distant, too remote, too much of a thrill seeker. Around for a good time, but beyond that, no one wanted to bother digging beneath the surface. I knew I wasn't easy. I didn't offer my heart on my sleeve for just anyone.

My phone buzzed, and I jumped for the distraction.

For as fluffy as clouds look, did you know they're heavy?

I snorted. August was full of odd facts and random comments, and I loved that I never knew what he would say next. I shot him back a message

Did you need to factor in weight for cloud-napping?

The dot-dot-dot was instantaneous.

The only napping I'm going to be doing with clouds is on them.

The smile rose within me unbidden, all storms dissipating. August had that effect on me, and I'd be lying if I said I didn't crave it. The more time I spent around him, the more I wanted him to be mine.

"Who's making you smile?" Serena asked, trying to peer over at my phone.

I slipped it back in my pocket, not wanting her to see our text chain. Panic rushed through me. Normally, I would've coasted through this family dinner, but tonight, I was close to stepping on minefields at every turn.

She arched her brow. "That was a heart-eyes look, Drake Castillo. You don't do heart eyes."

"Please tell me you're not dropping those terms in the courtroom." I deflected, even though I didn't stand a chance of her giving up. The bulldog had caught the scent, and while she might not push now, she wouldn't let this go.

Which meant I needed to sort my shit out when it came to August.

Whether that meant risk everything and claim him or end this, I still hadn't figured.

All I knew was I'd gotten myself in far too much trouble.

Chapter Thirteen

August

I'd been waiting for this client appointment all day.

Once I realized Ethan was the frontrunner of the band Drake wanted to book for his fundraiser, I was excited for the chance to help. I leaned forward, settling the paper in front of me in my booth at the shop. Drake's fundraiser wasn't for another few months, so there was a good chance Ethan could fit the performance into his band's schedule.

Even if I might not be around to see it.

The thought of moving made my heart squeeze tight. I'd been attempting the fingers in my ears "la, la, la" method of problem-solving, which meant I'd barely mulled it over. Not like I could bring up the issue to my friends here. They'd try to convince me to stay, just like Mom and Dad were trying to convince me to go.

And then I'd be more confused.

The one sway factor right now was Drake Castillo.

Was it healthy basing my life decisions on a guy I'd just started hooking up with? No, not in the slightest. But I'd never been considered healthy anyway.

My phone buzzed with a text from Mom.

This flower looks like it's frowning.

I snorted and started to type a message back and then stopped. The first thing that popped into my head was that the flower was one from the front yard that wouldn't be my parents' front yard anymore, and ugh. I sent a heart back instead of my usual rambling and set to my canvas.

I put the brush to paper, and blue bloomed on the sheet. Painting with watercolors offered a steady hit of dopamine, and I needed it bad. Mom and Dad had been sending me emails of rentals down in Florida. Truthfully, I hated all of them.

The stroke of purple burst on the page, the bright color against stark white reassuring in a way little else was. The sunset by a pier was a piece that had been cycling through my head ever since that night. Something about the clear lines of the shadowed pier, the crisp salt breeze making my head spin, and the pure magic that had dwelled between Drake and I during the show had stuck with me.

Finding that sort of chemistry was rare.

Rarer even to find chemistry that spanned beyond a single night.

I chewed on my lower lip as I coaxed more color onto the page.

"New painting?" Caspian asked, hovering over my stall. His shock of bright orange hair fit his temperament perfectly, a frequent comment he hated. Even though he was all scowls and crossed arms, he was a secret softy. Not as cuddly as Owen, but prickly like a hedgehog.

"Yeah, I've got a little bit before my next one," I said, returning my focus to the page.

"Damn, that's good, Auggie," he said, letting out a low whistle. "Are you going to put that up for sale when you're done?"

"Not sure yet." Part of me wanted to give this to Drake, but was that too gooey? "Is it weird to give your fuck buddy a picture?"

Cas snorted. "It is if they think you're casual and you're all in, like usual."

"Rude," I said. "What if it was a tastefully painted dick?"

"Honestly, if dick pics were painted rather than shot, I'd much prefer receiving them," Cas said. "The amount of guys who think they have a quality cock when it's less than average is staggering."

"Ouch," I said. "No cock judgment."

"Disagree," he said. "You send me an unprompted cock pic, and I'll judge the fuck out of it."

I snorted. "So if I send you one, I'll get a full analysis? Is it like divination of the cock? Cocktomancy?"

"Whoa, who's doing Cocktomancy?" Rory asked, swinging in. He perched on the edge of my desk and swung his legs back and forth.

"Don't you have clients?" Cas snarked.

Rory lifted his middle finger. "Don't be mad because I'm more efficient than you, Mr. Meticulous."

"Pretty sure that's a good trait for a tattoo artist," Caspian responded, his tone cracker-dry.

"Might just be because piercings are faster than tattoos," I suggested, cutting through this before they bickered for the next hour. Rory and Cas would pick a topic and roll. Arguing was a sport for them.

"Where have you been lately?" Rory asked, switching the topic at a whiplash pace. "I noticed you didn't come home the other night."

I wrinkled my nose. Fuck, I didn't even know what was going on between Drake and I other than really hot sex. We talked every day and were already making plans around our schedules to fit in time whenever we could. My pitiful heart whirred in overdrive.

"Would no comment work?" I asked, knowing it wouldn't. "Look, I'm not even in a position to be chasing a relationship."

"But you're two seconds away from proposing," Cas teased, a glint in his eyes.

I flipped him the middle finger and placed my paintbrush down. "I don't even know if I'll be here at the end of the year, so getting into a relationship isn't a great plan. Plus, he's my ex's brother, and I'm pretty sure there's a law against that or something."

"Unless you're in a throuple with the siblings, you're not breaking any laws," Cas argued. "And I guess since you wouldn't be the one incest-ing, it still wouldn't be breaking any?"

"Wait, wait, wait," Rory said. "What the fuck are you talking about? Whether you'll be here or not?"

Oh, shit. Me and my big mouth.

"Look, nothing is decided, but my folks want me to move down to Florida with them," I muttered.

"I thought you didn't want to?" Rory asked, his brows drawing together. I could hear the upset bubbling in his voice because he was shit at hiding his emotions, even though he deflected like a motherfucker.

I scrubbed my face. Ugh, this was too complicated to peel open. And I hadn't even brought up the Drake factor. Rory wasn't wrong. I didn't want to. I liked living in the Northeast. But I couldn't dispel the fear that everyone was going to leave me if I stayed. Folks moved on from work. Rory would move out. And it wasn't like I'd had any luck in finding a lasting partner.

"I have no idea what I want," I groaned.

"Except for your ex's brother," Caspian teased, offering an out. "Don't think I missed that tidbit."

"Wait, I did," Rory said, switching directions at once. "Shit, is he hot?"

"Tattooed fireman," I said with a shrug. "I'm not sad."

Rory's jaw dropped. "No way. You're the most chill guy ever. How are you involved in something scandalous like that?"

"Is it?" I asked. "It wasn't like I broke up with Serena or cheated on her or anything."

Cas snorted. "Only you, babe." He took a step away. "Time for me to get back to my stall and catch up on sketch work. Hope your sorry ass knows the place wouldn't be the same without you. So, if you leave for fucking Florida, I'll place a hex on your family."

"Thanks, I think?" I wrinkled my nose.

"August, your client's here," Nyx yelled from her stall farther down.

Rory let out a huff as he hopped up from his perch. "Don't think you've heard the end of this from me."

"I know," I muttered, cleaning my paintbrushes. I could continue the piece later. Rory giving me hell was only because he cared, and I loved how fierce of a fuck he gave.

Right now, I had a client, the one I'd been waiting for. I hopped up from my stall and went up front to find Ethan sitting on the couch, flipping through one of the art books we had on the coffee table. We were in the middle of a piece for him, so I'd be adding color today, which would be a long session. I loved the mixture of unique fish he wanted in an oceanscape, so different from the normal koi sleeves people got. Seeing him now was kind of jarring after watching him perform, that person entirely different.

He was an attractive guy with black gauges, dark black hair, and pretty blue eyes—just missing the eyeliner. Cas had checked him out, same as Owen, but I was so damn hung up on Drake that nothing else sparked my libido. Clearly, a problem for future me to deal with.

"Hey," I called out. "Come on back."

He pushed up from his seat and flashed me a grin. "Sick of seeing me yet?"

"Add one more to the tally," I said. "I saw you guys play earlier in the week."

Ethan's eyes widened. "No way, really? Why didn't you come up and say hi?"

Heat rushed through me at the memory. Mostly because Drake and I had been desperate to fuck. I squeezed my nape. "My friend had invited me out. He's looking for talent for a firehouse fundraiser and had his eye on you guys."

"You told him we'd play, right?" Ethan asked, excitement brimming from him. "I've never done a firehouse gig, but I feel like that'd be fun as hell."

"Don't you all need to confirm dates and stuff?" I asked, my brow wrinkling.

Ethan let out a bark of laughter. "Right, that. That's why we have Jesse. I'll call him and ask, but if you don't have the fundraiser dates nailed down yet, yeah. We're in. I've got personal reasons for wanting to support the firehouse."

"Shit, that easy is it?" I teased as I guided him back to my station where I'd be continuing the color work on his arm. Ethan settled into the seat, and I checked over my tray to make sure everything was stocked, from Vaseline to paper towels. "Nothing's changed on the design front, right?"

Ethan shook his head. "Nah, same as what we discussed last time. I want the watercolor feel to the piece. Can't wait to see how this turns out."

Once upon a time, I'd been nervous when clients shared their hopes with me about pieces, wondering if my work or artistic vision would hold up, if they'd be disappointed in the aftermath. However, after a few years in the field, all that remained was the pure joy of getting to create. Of the expression that tattooing allowed. And this place, Owen's tutelage, had helped me thrive in a way beyond what I could've imagined.

Sure, the occasional grump still came through the door, but the more I cultivated a book of regulars, the less frequent that became. Which was something I wouldn't have if I moved to Florida. I swallowed the lump in my throat.

I went through the usual motions to prep the area, then sat down beside him and got my tattoo gun. The first color we'd start with was blue, since it'd be the predominant color of the piece. I dipped the tip into the ink and turned the machine on. The gun buzzed in my hand, the hum a comfort I craved.

Right here and now, the confusion that had been plaguing me melted away.

"Ready?" I asked as I poised the tip over his skin. "Tell me all about the next gig you've got coming up."

"Next week," he said. "I can't wait."

While he talked about his hopes, dreams, and future, I set the needle to skin and got to work.

***

Ethan's piece took the next three hours, and by the time I finished, I was ready to crash with a beer back at my house. My hand had a bit of a cramp to it, and I massaged it while cleaning up my station. Every surface and tool needed to be sterilized, so this was a painstaking but necessary process.

I cast a quick glance to my phone. During the break we'd taken mid-session, I'd shot the news to Drake about Ethan being willing to play his fundraiser. He hadn't texted back yet, but I was desperate to talk to him. To see him.

Which all spelled bad news for my heart.

Despite going into this with my mindset latched on hookup, I clearly hadn't followed my own advice or direction.

A loud, ear-piercing alarm rang out.

I dropped the crumpled paper towel I was holding at once. The sound of a fire alarm had been ingrained in me from an early age, and my legs carried me forward even as my mind caught up.

"What's going on?" Nyx asked as she rushed up to my side.

"No idea, but we better get out," I said. "Who else is in here?"

"Just us and Owen. Clients are all gone for the day."

"I'll call," Nyx said, whipping out her phone and dialing the fire department.

We reached the front of Alchemy Ink, but I didn't spot Owen outside. My heart thumped hard, and I sucked in a breath, trying to suss out any scent of smoke in the air, a hint of fire. Owen came rushing up through the main area.

"Come on," Nyx said, holding the door open. "Out, out, out."

We rushed out of Alchemy Ink, my heart in my throat.

I couldn't lose this place.

Chapter Fourteen

Drake

The second we got the call, I launched into action, pulling on all my turnout gear and heading for the truck.

My adrenaline kicked in, but this time, the nerves did too.

The site of the call was Alchemy Ink. August's job.

Even though I lived in the area and knew plenty of people in it, I wasn't used to rushing to calls where someone I cared about might be involved. A cold sweat broke out on my forehead. I sure as fuck didn't like it.

The sirens blared as Dooley drove, cutting through the streets at top speed. Couldn't be fast enough.

We'd had a light day, yet it was still consumed with small instances of running out to handle small situations, more rescue efforts than fires. Which was fine by me, as the past few shifts had been exhausting.

A fire alarm had turned on, but the caller hadn't specified a fire. I held onto the hope it was just a faulty wire that had tripped or something insignificant. Was he working? I thought he was working today, but maybe he'd already left. Still, we couldn't get there fast enough. I clutched tight to the bar as we flew through another stoplight, the steady blare of the alarms an internal metric of my own fear. My mouth was dry. Fuck.

Dooley turned a corner hard, and I tightened my hold on the bar. The last time I'd seen August, he'd been sex and sleep rumpled and splayed out in my bed. Gorgeous as hell and with an easy smile I wanted to memorize. The last thing I wanted to see was the flicker of flames when we reached the end of the block. My gut soured. Damn it.

My focus zeroed in on getting to Alchemy Ink as fast as damn possible.

Hannigan stood across from me, not the person I'd have picked to be here while I was having an internal freakout. He'd been grating all day, and I couldn't very well tell him the guy I was sort of seeing might be at the building we were headed toward. My palms grew sweaty inside my gloves, and I closed my eyes, focusing on leveling out my breathing before we arrived on the scene.

The truck braked to a halt.

I launched into action at once. My boots landed on the asphalt with a thud, and I raced around the side of the truck at the same time Dooley emerged from the front. Hannigan's footsteps thudded behind me as the three of us raced up to assess the scene.

Not a hint of smoke marred the air, which was crisp and clear.

Three figures stood by one of the cars.

Even though my adrenaline was surging, I could see there weren't any signs of dangerous levels of fire. An older guy approached us with a wave, and the other two followed behind him.

"I'm so fucking sorry," he said the moment he came within range. "I'm Owen, the owner. My employee called when the alarm sounded."

"Pretty normal protocol," I joked.

The guy standing behind Owen emerged, and relief slammed full force into me.

August Jones.

Holy shit, he was safe. My shoulders relaxed, even though I hadn't realized they'd been hiked up.

"Drake, is that you?" he asked as he closed the distance. The urge to crush him to my body and claim those gorgeous lips, rose up fast and fierce inside me. His blond hair was swept to the side, and his meandering saunter was so damn attractive, like he was never in a rush.

"What's going on with the fire?" Hannigan called out. "We're not here to chat."

Fucking asshole.

Owen clutched his nape and ducked his head. "Fucking dumbest reason. I was sneaking a smoke too close to the alarm."

The woman slapped him on the shoulder. "No one's going to criticize you for struggling. Stop being all furtive and shit."

"Furtive is his modus operandi, Nyx," August joked.

I breathed easier. "So, no fire?"

"No fire," Owen said. "I'm so sorry for wasting all your time. I'll donate extra at the next fundraiser."

Dooley let out a bark of a laugh. "No need to apologize. I'd way rather be here for a mistake than a huge ass fire. You guys do good work. My grandma got her first tattoo with you."

August stepped closer to me, and even though there were only a few feet between us, it felt like miles. I ached to reach out and wrap him in my arms, to touch him in some way, but we were in front of our coworkers. I wasn't even sure what he wanted at this point—or what I even wanted.

All I knew was that the draw to him had become so magnetic, I hadn't been able to stay away.

Even if I'd left more of my sister's questions unanswered.

"Two fires in a month," I teased August. "Better put you on a warning registry."

"Look, the kitchen fire might've been my fault, but this wasn't," he said, lifting his palms up. "I wasn't the one secret-smoking in the back."

"I'm assuming I'm never going to live this down," Owen muttered.

"Mostly because a. you should know better, and b. none of us are going to give you shit for having a stressful week and caving." The other tattoo artist passed him a rueful look as she shook her head.

"I'm going to wait in the truck," Hannigan said, being a brat as he stormed off. Because he couldn't be professional for a hot second.

"What's his problem?" the chick asked.

"Existence?" I shrugged. "He's been a little bitch all day." Dooley snort-laughed.

"I'm guessing you didn't get my text?" August asked.

"You guys know each other?" Owen asked, glancing between us, a discerning look in his eyes.

"Uh, yeah," I said, not knowing how to fill in the blank. "We're concert buddies."

"That what they calling it nowadays?" Dooley muttered under his breath. I elbowed him in the side. He'd caught me texting August a few times and had interrogated me. Mostly because he was a nosy sonofabitch. I might've caved because Dooley was a good fucking friend, and I needed to talk to someone about this shit.

"Why don't we go in and inspect the building while we're here," I suggested, to avoid the stares on us right now. "Dot the I's and all that."

"Hannigan can sulk in the truck," Dooley said, taking the lead toward the front of the building.

August stepped in line with me, and I made sure to not-accidentally bump elbows with him. He glanced up, an unguarded grin on his gorgeous face that knocked the breath from me. His long lashes, his sprinkling of a few dark freckles despite his tanned skin, and his dimples made my heart race.

"What was in your text?" I asked as we walked in time with each other, and I tried to ignore the stares of his two coworkers behind us. If gossip flew here like it did at the firehouse, they'd be grilling him before we left.

"Ethan was my last client before all this nonsense," he said, waving his hand around to gesture at the fire alarm still blaring. The sound was familiar for me at this point, fading to background noise. I especially didn't mind when the emergency call ended up being a non-emergency. Knowing August was safe calmed me, and the severity of my reaction delivered some stronger truths than I was ready to navigate.

Like the fact I really wanted to date him.

"Ethan?" I asked, following Dooley to the back where the alarm was. "One second. We'll turn this off so we can discuss."

I stepped up next to Dooley, and we shut off the fire alarm, then checked around the area for any signs of smoke or fire that might've gone undetected. Sure, fire alarms could be triggered for stupid reasons, but occasionally they went off for other reasons, and I didn't want to put anyone here at risk due to distracted negligence. The routine calmed me like nothing else.

"All clear," Dooley said, then glanced to Owen. "Mind if I take a look at the art you've got up front?" He passed me a wink, and gratitude soaked through me. Clearly, he was giving me and August a second to catch up.

Dooley, Owen, and Nyx headed up to the front, leaving August and me in the back room.

The air crackled with tension between us.

Fuck it.

I closed the distance between us and slammed my lips to his. I drank August in like fresh, cool water after a three-alarm fire. The relief that rushed through me, fast and furious, was telling of how far gone I was for this man. The way he melted against me, how he met me with the same intensity I'd craved. August was everything I never thought I'd find, and I hated the circumstances on how we met.

That he was my sister's ex-boyfriend.

That didn't stop me from wanting him, body and soul.

I wove my fingers through his hair, our bodies slamming together—at least as much as they could in my turnout gear. Fuck, he was so pliable, so sweet, so addictive. August let out a low moan, the vibration reverberating through me. For the short time since we'd gotten the call, I'd been worried as fuck, and if anything, that cemented these feelings for him weren't just sprouting to wither—no, they were taking root.

My heart rate slowed as our kisses grew less desperate, and I savored the taste of him, the plushness of his lips. Except I was on the clock, and guaranteed Hannigan was sitting in the truck ready to pitch a fit. I pulled away from him, a sigh escaping me.

"Sorry if I crossed any lines with coworkers," I offered. "Wasn't sure how to handle the situation."

August snorted. "Me neither, so concert buddies works for me. They're a nosy bunch."

"What were you going to tell me earlier?"

August's face burst into a huge smile, radiant like the dawn. "Spring Fires is in. Ethan was my last client, and not only did he speak for the band there, but he said he had a personal reason for wanting to support the firehouse."

I blinked at August. "No shit, really?" Excitement trickled through me, and I wrapped my hands around his hips and lifted him up. My lips found him again before I settled him on his feet again.

"Well, damn, that was hot," August said, fanning himself. "We're the same size."

I shrugged. "We've got to be physically ready for the job. Why, you want me to lift you up some other time?" My voice lowered with intent, and August's nostrils flared.

"Fuck yes, please," he said. "I'd probably paint the wall with jizz."

A bright laugh burst out of me, ones that came easily around him. "Thank you for asking him. You didn't have to do that."

"I wanted to," August said. "You're passionate about this, and I want to see if the concert fundraiser trumps spaghetti dinner."

My heart squeezed tightly. He offered his support as if that wasn't a rare and beautiful thing. With August, I'd been entertaining a different fantasy as of late—the kind involving evenings together and subsequent sunrises. Of dinners out and slumping on the couch together after long days. Of a relationship instead of flings, something I thought wasn't in the realm of possibility.

"Are you free tomorrow night?" I asked. "I'm done in the morning, need to crash out for a bit, but I'm around after."

"Yeah, actually," he said. "What do you have in mind?"

"A date," I offered, my heart thumping a little harder. He might hate the idea, blanch at it, and I'd just backtrack. But hell, I needed to try. "If you want."

His eyes widened, those hazel eyes gorgeous, and his grin somehow grew a little brighter. "Yeah, I do. Tell me when and where, and I'll be there."

Elation flooded through me.

I leaned in and pressed a quick kiss to his lips. "I have to go before Hannigan storms in to complain, but I'll see you tomorrow."

This wouldn't be easy—I still hadn't addressed the Serena of the situation. But I also wasn't ready to pass on a chance for more with this gorgeous man either.

Tomorrow, we'd go on a date, and I'd see if this was a false start or could turn into a steady flame.

Chapter Fifteen

August

Yesterday had been a roller-coaster, what with the whole accidental fire emergency and Drake showing up at my job.

And damn, he looked fine in his turnout gear. Granted, he looked fine every time I ran into him.

I've been waiting all day for our date tonight. I'd woken up to a text with the time and place—five pm at Chickies Rock Overlook, out in Lancaster. Not close, but an easy drive. I hadn't been there before, but I loved surprises, so this pinged my excitement in the best way. Especially the fact he'd called it a date when he asked.

Which had to mean either he was interested in more or he was really formal about his friend meetups. But who knew. Maybe he meant a concert buddy date. A bro-tastic good time. Ugh, I hoped not.

I wanted to suck his dick, but romantically.

I zoomed down the highway toward Lancaster, all pastures and deep blue skies during the pre-evening hour. The sun's golden rays lit up fields of wheat, the perfect lighting enhancing the gorgeous peacefulness out here. At least when it wasn't interrupted by some super preachy billboard about getting with Jesus or hating on babies, I think? The slogans were never quite clear. The breeze filtered in, bringing the smell of sweet, fresh-cut grass and cow shit. Obviously, one was preferable to the other.

Mom and Dad were away right now, checking out a prospective property in Florida, and they kept sending me pictures, which I love/hated. I loved the attention, but I hated the subtle pressure because they really wanted me to join them.

I was pushing off processing what I wanted to do on that front, even though Rory had started to poke at me. Sooner than later, he'd corner me, and I'd have to sort out what I wanted. The thought of leaving Drake right as we were exploring whatever this was tore at my insides, but if I was wrong, like I often was, I'd just end up left in the dirt.

I turned up the volume of the Sleeping Fires playlist I was listening to. The band was damn good, and I was stoked Drake was talking with Ethan to figure out the date for the fundraiser.

I took the exit off the highway and headed in the direction of Chickies Rock Overlook, catching a few of the signs for it. Wild that I'd lived in the area and hadn't been here. Drake had a sense of adventure that I craved. He was the guy who suggested a midnight drive to nowhere and dove headfirst into putting out fires, and god, I hadn't realized how much I wanted someone like that until I experienced it. Every time we met up, my creative mind sparked into overdrive, inspiration flowing better than it had in years. The one watercolor piece was finished, and I was already working on another.

I pulled into the parking lot, and a brief scan rewarded me with the sight of Drake's car, so I snagged the spot beside it.

When I hopped out of my car, his driver's side door creaked open. The sight of him caused the breath to snag in my throat. Drake was dressed in a black muscle tee that showed off his defined biceps and forearms and threadbare jeans with a few rips. His backwards ball cap was hot as hell, and I wanted to drop to my knees and suck him off right there in the parking lot.

He let out a low whistle. "Damn, you look good."

Heat rushed through me at the compliment. I'd thrown on a pair of cargo shorts that made my ass pop and a salmon tank top, which Rory often referred to as my slutty little tank top. Maybe because I hoped to get laid tonight. Drake's eyes were molten as he scanned over me, and he licked his lips, the hunger in his expression palpable.

"Man, the plan is a hike, but you're pure temptation," he said, his voice growing low.

"I'd say I'd blow you on the hike, but I'm pretty sure we'd be tempting fate," I said, glancing at all the cars in the lot.

Drake snorted and extended his hand. I settled my palm in his, a thrill rising inside me feeling him hold my hand. Such a simple thing, but I was so used to partners who were minimal PDA or not nearly as invested as I was.

"Come on," he said, giving my hand a light tug. "The entrance is this way."

We set off on the trail, trees looming overhead. The air was crisp, lush from the forests around us. I hadn't gotten out to just hike in a while, and it felt good, especially after spending yesterday hunched over and tattooing. I needed the movement.

"So, I think Ethan and I hammered out the date for the fundraiser," Drake said, his eyes gleaming as we walked hand in hand down the trail. My gaze kept drifting to where our hands were joined. A part of me couldn't believe the way he publicly claimed me like this. Especially after yesterday, when he'd declared us "concert buddies" in front of our coworkers.

Not like Owen or Nyx had believed that for a second.

"Hope you're going to clue me in so I can be there," I said, even though the thought of future planning tangled my insides. If I moved, I might not be. And if I stayed, I'd disappoint my parents.

"Baby, you'll be the first to know," Drake said, giving my hand a squeeze. He flashed me an incandescent grin, the wicked arch of his brows, the sparkle in his eyes only making him hotter. The term of endearment sent a flush right through me. "My message probably would've been left unread if you hadn't asked Ethan."

"He's a great client," I said with a shrug. "The piece we're working on right now is a lot of fun."

"Your specialty?" he asked.

"Yeah, it's watercolor," I responded, even though more questions bubbled up on my tongue that I swallowed down. Did he want this to be more as much as I did? Would he be okay telling Serena, even though we'd dated? Did he want me to stay?

The setting shifted around us, the trees interspersed by more and more jutting rock the farther down the trail we strolled. People walked by on either side, some coming, some going. A few were jogging, others moseying like we were. Being with Drake felt endless, like time stilled and we existed in this stasis, everything else melting away.

I'd fallen before, but never like this.

The way he moved with confidence and surety, how he looked forward rather than down—everything about him drew me in.

"Did Hannigan get pissy over the call?" I asked, needing to blurt out something that wasn't all the feelings building inside me.

Drake let out a low whistle. "When isn't he pissy? I don't know what his damage is, if he's in the wrong field or what, but yeah, in the year I've known him, he's had like three good days."

"Our resident grump isn't really that way," I said. "Cas is all teeth but no bite."

"Seems like you have a close crew at Alchemy Ink."

My chest squeezed tight. As much as Mom and Dad swore they'd found some great tattoo shops, I couldn't imagine stumbling onto one like this. We were a puppy pile of misfits who scrambled all over each other, and I wouldn't have it any other way.

"Yeah, Owen keeps accumulating us," I joked. "We're a part of his collection."

"Oh? Is there something..." Drake asked, his grip on my hand tightening.

I wrinkled my nose. "Something what?"

"Between you and Owen?"

The laugh burst out of me. "Oh god, no. He's the sweetest guy on the planet, don't get me wrong, but the relationships I have with the folks from work are more like family."

Admitting that out loud settled something inside me I hadn't realized had been cracked open. No wonder my current situation felt like a divorce. Because either choice I made, I'd be separated from family.

My phone buzzed, and I slipped it out to check—more texts from my parents. A sigh escaped me.

"Everything okay?" Drake asked.

"Gumdrops and butterflies," I blurted out. Right, that was believable.

Drake arched an eyebrow, his steady glance on me giving enough pressure that I caved.

"Fine, so I know I mentioned my folks are selling their house, but they're moving all the way down to Florida, and I hate it," I admitted. Things between Drake and I were so tentative, so new, that I didn't want to drop the fact they wanted me to come with them too. "They're sending me pictures of the area."

He squeezed my hand, a reminder ours were clasped, and warmth rippled through me. This was the support from a partner I'd craved my entire life, and I didn't want to run away from it.

"Did it come out of nowhere?" he asked.

"Yeah," I muttered. "Probably why I'm still struggling to process any of it."

"I'd be thrown if any of my family were moving," Drake said, broaching what had felt like an off-limits topic until now. That I'd dated his sister first had been something we'd carefully danced around.

"You guys are close, right?" Jealousy twisted my insides. As an only child, a part of me had always wanted a sibling, even though everyone I talked to about it swore there were pros and cons.

"We are," Drake said, trailing off.

I squeezed his hand back. "Sounds real convincing there."

He heaved out a breath and stared up at the sky, which was partially obscured by all the trees and their branches slicing into the blue expanse. "Serena and Blair have always been easy successes. Excelled in school and socially, then went on to become a lawyer and a doctor. We're close, but fuck, it's hard not to get lost in the comparison game."

I wrinkled my nose. "What about hottie firefighter doesn't say success?"

He flashed me a heated look. "I'm not used to anyone viewing me that way."

The realization settled in me slowly as we walked along the dirt path, the stone rising on either side of us as we neared the overlook. "That's why the fundraiser's so important to you, isn't it?"

He let out a soul-weary sigh that sounded like it had been trapped inside him. "Dumb, right? Close to thirty and I'm still trying to shout "look at me" to my folks."

I shook my head. "Not dumb at all. But if it makes any difference, when it comes to you, I can't look away." Admitting that truth aloud sent a frisson of vulnerability through me. This was when I threw myself in too deep and scared them away. But the slight bunch of Drake's shoulders, the fragile air of his admission that surrounded him spurred me on regardless.

"You're one of a kind, August Jones," he murmured, a reverence in his voice that made me glow.

Up ahead, rocks clustered around the trail, which ended at the overlook. People stood at the guardrails along the edge, staring out into the distance. Both of us lapsed into quiet as we made our way along the rockier terrain, climbing up larger stone slabs to reach the higher ground. The closer we got, the more glittering glimpses of the Susquehanna River appeared into view.

"Have you been here before?" I asked as we neared, bypassing a few folks lounging comfortably on the rocks, enjoying the waning sunlight and warmth.

"Not for a long while," Drake said. "Figured it was about time to head out this way again."

We scaled one of the larger slabs that led to the edge, and Drake stepped up first and offered a boost over the slight jump to the higher spot. Once I settled onto the surface and stared out past the overlook, my breath snagged in my throat. The deep golds and oranges of the evening sun licked over the ripples of water below, and from this high up, I could see miles down the river.

"Damn," I swore as I watched the beginnings of the sunset coast over the skyline. The pristine clouds grew gilt edges, and magenta and burnished orange streaks tumbled lazily across the horizon. Drake stood still beside me, our hands intertwined, even though they'd become sweaty. His presence was solid, unwavering, and with him by my side, I found myself straightening up, facing what lay before me head on.

As if his bravery bolstered my own.

The sweetened, crisp air traveled my way, and I sucked down a lungful, letting it circulate through me, lifting me higher with every passing second.

I'd witnessed many sunsets in my lifetime, but a profoundness settled inside me with this one. Like this would be emblazoned in my memories for the rest of my days. Drake's hand rested in mine, and I'd never felt so connected to another person before. We stood side by side, witnessing this majesty together, but the skin-to-skin connection elevated the grandeur even more. As if we weren't two sentinels but twined together with the promise of something unbreakable.

Something I'd always longed for.

I wasn't sure if minutes or hours passed as the sky blazed in its natural parade, the sun gliding beneath the horizon in one last glorious burst of light. The colors reflected over the Susquehanna below, amplifying all that beauty, and I soaked in every last detail. Even the other people watching were hushed, speaking in murmurs, if they did at all. The sunset had stolen everyone's attention with the breathtaking show only nature could deliver.

The air cooled as the light faded, and I leaned closer to Drake, so our arms brushed together, the contact sending electricity through me. I didn't want to budge as the sun careened beneath the horizon and left the beginning salvo of night. The shadows deepened, darkening our features, and even that left me with a quiet sense of beauty I hadn't been able to access before.

Even though my mind had been a tangled mess before, right here and now, it grew silent, and I accepted the gift.

I was also well aware who was the cause.

I took the chance and leaned in closer until I rested against him. He extricated our hands, and a minute later, his arm wrapped around my shoulders as he brought me in, close to him. The scent of cedar and smoke caressed me, his furnace heat intoxicating. I could live in this moment for a lifetime.

If that was any indication, I'd already started to fall for Drake Castillo.

Chapter Sixteen

Drake

When I stepped inside my house, I kicked my shoes off and flicked the lights on. My heart thudded hard with anticipation. I wasn't going to be alone tonight.

After the date at Chickies Rock Overlook, I'd taken August to grab takeout, and we'd scarfed down cheesesteaks while sitting at the picnic tables outside of Jerry's Deli. The tension between us grew with every passing second, closer to implosion. And when I invited him over, the heat ratcheted up a thousand degrees.

A knock sounded at the door, and I spun around to backtrack.

When I drew the door open, August stood waiting in the frame, and my breath caught. His blond strands were wind-tousled, his lips lush and reddened, and the way his tank top flirted with his nipples drew my eyes. Combined with the shorts that showcased his supple ass, and August was a smokeshow.

"C'mere," I said, grabbing him by the flimsy tank and dragging him forward. Our lips crashed together, and all the tension that had been brewing between us, an intoxicating combination of lust and sweetness, descended.

Every word that passed between us tonight had tightened those threads that ensnared me until I never wanted to let go.

His mouth was hungry and eager, getting me hotter with every kiss. I savored the taste of him, the crispness of the beer we drank, and the softness of his lips. The heat of him was addictive. I wanted to taste him all over, to map his skin with my mouth.

We pulled back for breath, and his eyes were shiny, wild with lust. "Fuck, I want your cock."

I licked my lips. I was vers but preferred to top, and I'd clearly met my perfect match. "Can I have yours after?"

August's eyes widened, and a grin spread across his lips. "Hell yes."

"Whoever strips down first gets to fuck first," I proclaimed, tugging my shirt off. I dropped my pants and briefs to the floor and looked over at August, who fiddled with his shirt on purpose, an impish smirk on his lips.

"What?" he proclaimed. "I told you I wanted your cock."

I kicked off my socks and shoes, moving the rest of my stuff into a pile. "Well, if you want me to fuck you against this wall, you'd better be stripped by the time I grab a condom and lube."

"I just got tested," he said. "Waiting on results, but next time..."

I licked my lips. "You want me to take you bare?"

His nostrils flared, and he nodded.

Flames roared through me. "Yeah, I definitely want that. I'm negative on my tests, so once you get your results, I'll sink right inside that sweet ass." With that, I strode away from him and headed for the bathroom where I had lube and condoms stashed. I rummaged around, my cock thick, my balls heavy at the thought of the gorgeous man waiting for me.

I snagged what I needed and padded back into the living room, where August waited for me, completely stripped down. His body was stunning, a work of art. His arms were decked out, the healed Charmander on his bicep, the skull and crossbones on the other one. His forearms featured black and white tattoos of clocks with snakes wrapped around them. The lighthouse from his hips to ribs on his right offered a splash of color, and a few tendrils wrapped around his left thigh from the octopus he had along the side.

Beyond that, his blond hair was tousled, looking windswept, his nipples dark and mouthwatering, and his cock was fucking pretty, a nice firm length I couldn't wait to have buried inside me. August was lanky, but I'd picked him up before—he had some sexy-as-fuck definition to his physique. And goddamn, I couldn't wait to drive into him until we were boneless.

I wanted him to be mine.

Not a temporary fling. Not a hookup.

Mine.

I strode up to him and gripped his hip tightly, guiding him back toward the nearest wall. When his back thudded against the surface, I leaned in and pressed my lips to his. My cock brushed against his hip, his against mine, pre-cum smearing on skin. A shiver ran through me from our proximity, from this driving need to bury inside him. I wanted to feel him, wanted us to be connected in every damn way possible.

I kissed August while I ripped open the condom and rolled it onto my cock. Then I slathered my length with lube and reached between his legs, brushing past his soft balls to rub the rest of the lube across the tight ring of muscle there.

August let out a whimper against my mouth as I circled my fingers around his hole lazily, enjoying the tease. He tried to shift his hips, rubbing against my fingers, as if he wanted to spear himself on them. I slid my middle one in, the tight heat swallowing it up, and I gave him a few pumps.

"Fuck yes," he gasped, shifting up and down on my finger, my palm cradling his taint. I nipped and sucked at the column of his neck as he rode on my finger. I crooked it deep inside him, and he let out a sinful moan. "God, I want you inside me."

"Wrap your thighs around my waist," I said, tugging my finger out and grabbing him by the hips to help. August wrapped his arms around my shoulders, and I hiked him up to my waist, his thighs clamping around my hips. My cock slid between his cheeks, and I rocked back and forth, rubbing against his hole. He leaned against the wall, his hands braced on my shoulders, and I let go with one hand to line my cock up.

"Ready for me?" I asked, my core tensed to keep him upright.

"Beyond," he said, a breathiness to his voice that I adored.

I pushed my tip inside, his sweet heat nearly obliterating me. "Damn, baby, you feel like silk." I let out a deep groan and thrust in deeper. August's muscles relaxed at once, and the long, loud moan from him coaxed me farther. I sank all the way inside, buried to the hilt inside his tight hole. Sweat broke out on my forehead from how good he felt. August relaxed against the wall, and I shifted closer, so our bodies were pressed together, his cock brushing against my abs.

His grip on my shoulders tightened, his nails pricking into my skin. I moved my grasp on him to his thighs and dragged back to sink inside him again. Bliss rushed through me in a sinful sweep, and I savored the sensations. August gasped and tilted his head back, his Adam's apple bobbing with a sharp swallow. I began to fuck him in earnest, finding my rhythm. Each squeeze of his tight hole around my cock brought me close to the brink already. My balls were heavy with an unrelenting ache. Having August in my arms like this—fuck, I wanted to unload into him bare. Watch my cum drip from him, lap it up after.

"You're so good for me," I murmured. "So fucking sweet."

A full-body shiver rolled through him as I continued fucking into his hole, shallow strokes that sent me to heaven every damn time. His moans were explosive, growing louder by the second. His pre-cum smeared all over my stomach from the way his hard length brushed against me on every thrust. August clenched hard to me, and while he wasn't light, he was easy enough to lift given the weight I was used to managing from work. And hell, having him in my arms like this, ramming into him up against the wall, was a fantasy brought to life.

"Oh god," he moaned. "Take me apart."

I sank my teeth into his shoulder, tasting the salt of his sweat, and I fucked into him with hard and sharp strokes. The gasps and moans that burst from him were so loud they echoed around the room, and I drank them in. God, the way his hole felt squeezing around my cock, the seductive glide whenever I thrust in—I could live here, connected to him. Every time we fucked, I wanted more, and if that wasn't a sign August was someone I shouldn't let go, I didn't know what was.

"Damn, I want to stay in your hole all night. Just fuck you to sleep, my cum buried in you," I said, the imagery burning me hotter. "And then fuck you awake, only to spill into you all over again. You'll be leaking my cum for days."

"Oh god," August gasped, a sharp urgency in his tone. "If you want me to last, you'd better stop talking like that."

"You want that, baby?" I teased as I fucked into him steadily, addicted to the smooth glide. My balls grew heavy, the tension increasing with every thrust. "My cock in your mouth, in your hole, every chance we get?"

A whimper sounded from him, and a thrill whispered through me. If that was a fantasy of his, I'd happily make it come true. If I had him in my life, in my home, I wouldn't be able to stop from sliding into him constantly, if only to watch the sweet surrender on his features.

I nipped along his neck as my pace increased, those sharp, short strokes dragging me closer and closer to the edge. Sweat trickled down my back as my thighs burned from holding him upright like this, a similar burn in my forearms. Not like I cared. I could pay for it tomorrow, but having August in my arms, fucking him up against my wall was worth any aches.

My heart ran rampant, wild and uncontrolled as I fucked him like I'd never get the chance again. A frenzy claimed my movements as I rammed into him over and over again, our moans and cries growing louder. The skin-to-skin sensations pushed me into overdrive, the chemistry between us undeniable. I'd never connected with anyone the way I did with him, and I never wanted this to end.

My breaths came faster, sweat rolling down my forehead with a tickle as the tension gripped me so hard I could focus on little else. So. Damn. Close.

His hole gripped me tight with each glide, and as I slid in again, all the pressure tipped over.

My balls drew up, and I came hard.

My vision blanked, my grip on his thighs tightening, and my cum spilled from me in violent spurts. I sagged forward, crushing August against the wall as I tried to catch my breath, floating on the pleasure flooding through my limbs.

"Fuck," I swore, clutching onto him like a lifeline.

As I settled back to earth, I began to pull out of him, my cock already growing soft, and brought his legs down from my hips. Once he was settled on his feet, I tugged the condom off and tied it. His cock jutted out, desperate and needy, and August licked his lips as he gave it a stroke.

"Nope, none of that," I said. "You're going to come inside me."

My legs were a little shaky as I reached down to swipe the leftover condoms and lube, passing them over to August. When he grabbed them from me, I made my way over to my couch and bent over. "Want to take me here?"

"God, you're such a fantasy." August tore the packet and rolled the condom on. Then he strode over to the couch and dropped to his knees behind me. "I'm dying to come, but I want a taste of you first."

He leaned in and licked from taint to hole. The heat of his tongue, the wet glide, sent a burst of pure adrenaline through me. I hadn't been fucked in a long time, and it had been even longer since I'd been rimmed, but my limbs were lax and lazy in the wake of my release. August gave a few more exploratory licks before he gripped my cheeks hard.

Then he devoured.

My legs shook from the onslaught, his lips, tongue, teeth all working in unison to unmake me. I'd just come hard, but already, my cock started to stiffen again at the onslaught of pleasure as August ate me out like a fucking feast. I gripped the back of the sofa tightly, moans escaping me, first soft and then louder and louder. Spit dribbled down my thigh, but August didn't pause for air as he continued to lick and suck at my hole, the intensity increasing by the second.

Goddamn. August was a force, and I was helpless to resist him, whether it was being drawn to him or surrendering to him.

He pulled back, his breaths puffing against my hole. "Almost as delicious as your cock."

My length perked up, stiffening despite the orgasm he'd wrung from me. "Fuck me, baby," I murmured, thrusting my hips back. "Come inside me."

"Damn, this ass," August swore as he pushed up behind me. His hands circled around my hips, and he pried my cheeks open wide. His tip brushed against my hole. Normally, I'd need prep after such a long time, but he'd eaten me out so well I could easily take him. "You're going to feel amazing."

He began to push inside me, taking his time. There was a slight burn, a stretch there that I didn't mind. My muscles relaxed, and he slid deeper inside me, brushing against my prostate. Fireworks flared at the spot, a shot of pleasure straight into my veins.

"Goddamn." I'd forgotten how good it could feel to get fucked.

"Shit, you're so tight," he said. "Squeezing my dick. I'm not going to last long."

"Don't need you to," I gasped. "Just want to feel you moving inside me."

"I've got you," he said as his grip tightened around my hips. He drew back and pushed in again, and a long, low groan escaped me. August drew back again and thrust in, starting to find his rhythm. Pleasure flooded through me as he fucked me, a slow, luxurious push and pull. This wasn't a frenzied rush to completion but an exploratory glide as he sank into me. I gripped the back of the couch tightly to keep myself upright as I surrendered to the sensations.

My cock had grown hard, and a few droplets of pre-cum hit the floor as he fucked into me with a languorous rhythm that had me close to detonation again. He found my prostate with every stroke, and holy hell, I'd never had sex this explosive. I wanted his touch constantly, craved his presence like my next breath.

His breaths sawed from him, feverish, and the smacks of our skin echoed through the room. Sweat trickled down my back, beaded on the insides of my thighs as my balls ached and my cock bobbed with each movement. He thrust into me with a deliberateness that I felt deep in my core, a recognition there I'd been searching for. I'd been glossed over for years, but with August, he always seemed to see right through to the core of me.

As if I was the most important person in his view.

I didn't want to give that up. I couldn't.

"Oh fuck, I'm not going to last long," August gasped. "You're too damn tight. Fucking perfect."

"Come for me," I said, needing him to unleash.

August began to thrust in harder, faster, those smacks stinging with each collision. He brushed over my prostate each time, flicker-flares of pleasure bursting in me again and again. God, this man was everything I could've dreamed of.

"You're so fucking sexy," he murmured. "Fuck!"

He thrust in hard and stilled as his cum flooded into me, his cock pulsing with the streams. He collapsed onto me, his sweaty skin plastering against mine as his hands wrapped overtop of mine. For a few precious moments, we were just ragged breaths and serenity, the kind some spent a lifetime chasing.

August peeled away from me, even though I hated the space between us. He drew himself from my hole and tugged off the condom. I pushed up from the couch and ran my fingertips across my hole, the ache there fresh. I wanted to feel him for days.

He chewed on his lower lip and eyed my hard cock.

"Can I suck you off in bed?"

Fuck, he was a total dream.

I closed the distance between us and cupped his cheek. "Want to cockwarm me to sleep, baby?"

His eyes widened, his pupils dilating with lust. "Please."

"Come on," I said, stepping away but offering a hand out. August slid his into mine, and together, we walked in the direction of my bedroom. He peeled the condom off as we stepped inside and dropped it into my trash can. My sheets were rumpled, a handful of books stacked on my nightstand, mostly to-do guides on metal-crafting, which I'd wanted to get into for a while. I'd at least managed to sweep my pile of socks and dirty jeans into the hamper before having him over.

"Why's it so easy with you?" August asked, as if he plucked the question from my own head.

"Because I'm easy," I teased back, even though that felt off given the gravity that settled between us. "Maybe when you're around the right person, it isn't constant work. You can just... be."

And damn, didn't that sound like bliss.

"I always wanted that," August admitted, his voice small.

"Me too" rose to my lips but didn't escape. I wanted to ask him to be mine, to tell him how I felt so damn badly. I'd face Serena and whatever backlash that incurred. However, I'd been second-rate my whole life. What if we started dating, and he saw me differently? What if the glamor wore off, and I was just average? Nothing special.

Easy to leave.

I swallowed hard and settled into bed and tugged August in with me. He toppled over me, and we were a tangle of limbs, of skin, of heat. I kissed him for all I was worth, wishing, hoping he could somehow feel how much he meant to me through it. How his simple acceptance meant the world to me.

We kissed in my bed like the world was ending around us, and nothing else mattered.

August sprawled over me, and every point of contact, every brush of his body on mine, filled me with sparks. When he pulled away, he winked at me.

"Think you've got something that needs taking care of." He crawled farther down the bed, settling between my thighs, and swallowed me down in one gulp. A shout escaped me as his wet heat engulfed my sensitive cock.

August breathed through his nose as he choked on my cock, the splutter tightening his throat around my length. He bobbed up and down on my length, working me into a frenzy. I was already ignited from our kiss, from the touch, from him fucking me until I was unsteady, and it didn't take long until I was spilling down his throat.

I tilted my head back as cum shot from me, and August swallowed it all down. I ran my fingers through his blond strands, mesmerized by the sight of him, his lips wrapped around my cock. "Want to keep me nice and warm, baby?"

He let out a whimper.

"Let's shift a little and get comfortable," I said, keeping my palm on the back of his head as we shimmied down the bed and I rested my head on the pillow. August leaned his cheek against my thigh, settling there even while his mouth was still full of my cock. It had started to soften, but he gave it the occasional suck or kitten lick. His hazel eyes filled with bliss, a serenity there that made my heart squeeze tight. I settled back and stroked my fingers through his hair.

August's eyes fluttered closed, putting those long lashes on display. He sucked lightly on my cock again. The heat and connection to him better than I could've imagined. The wet warmth of his mouth was intoxicating, but I was beyond spent after two loads, one in each of his holes. I hadn't realized how much I craved contact until him, how much I'd been missing. Being with him offered a completeness I'd longed for my whole life.

Something I'd been chasing in every other direction, trying to find that thrill.

Turned out it waited here with August Jones.

His breaths grew more even as I continued to stroke his hair, even though his mouth didn't pull away from my cock.

My heart squeezed tight.

Fuck, I was in love.

Chapter Seventeen

August

The date with Drake had been utter perfection. I'd been thinking of it nonstop.

I'd done some errands, and when I pulled up to my house, Rory's car was parked out front, which meant he'd be home and full of questions. Though after last night, my mind wasn't as chaotic as it had been before.

One truth had emerged last night. Those bubbling feelings inside for Drake had solidified into something real. Something true.

I grabbed the handful of bags from the grocery store from the back and made my way to the front door.

The second I stepped inside, Rory exploded into view, all lanky limbs and accusations.

"August Evelyn Jones, I've been waiting for you."

The bags dropped from my hands and teetered to the side, the contents rolling out.

"My mangoes!" I dropped to the ground, trying to scoop them up before they escaped out the still-open door.

"Ah, shit, let me help." Rory chased an errant mango that had almost escaped and brought it over to the grocery bag. He lifted the bag up and strode toward the kitchen. "You're coming in here, August Henrietta Jones."

"You do know my middle name is Evan, right?" I muttered, dragging the other bag and my lightly bruised mangoes forward. I'd known from the moment I headed home that I was in for an interrogation, one I'd been avoiding all week. And my folks came home from their house-hunting trip to Florida tomorrow too. They'd be looking for answers from me. They had sent over an email with job listings, house listings, pretty much anything I'd need to move. They even included dentist recommendations and a selection of gay bars.

"Psh, you expect me to remember that?" Rory proclaimed as he set the bag on the kitchen counter.

"You remember my birthday. My middle name shouldn't be that hard."

"That's because it's your birthday." Rory leveled me a no-nonsense look. "Middle names are like taints, in between the important shit."

A laugh burst out of me, deflating some of the tension coiled inside. He was my best friend for a reason, and even though he might have some strong opinions about my plans, I knew in the end he'd support me no matter what.

"What the fuck are all these mangoes for?" Rory asked, picking up several from the bags and placing them on the counter.

"Eating? What the fuck else would they be for?"

"I don't know, some new figging fad?" Rory opened the fridge and jettisoned cheese, yogurts, and cherry tomatoes inside.

"Keep my mangoes far away from your ass," I said, clutching one protectively. "In fact, I think I'm going to carve some up now." I snagged a knife and cutting board and diced up a few of the mangoes while Rory put away the rest of the groceries. Within minutes, I'd accumulated a little pile of yellow-orange squares, and I popped them in a bowl and joined Rory over at the kitchen table.

The tension returned between us as I set the bowl on the table.

"So how was Drake's?" Rory asked. "Assuming that's where you were the other night?"

"Eat some damn mango," I muttered, pushing the bowl in his direction.

He rolled his eyes and popped a few cubes in his mouth. His nose wrinkled. "Wow, what a shitty fruit."

"More for me then," I said, snagging a few and savoring the sweet, sharp taste.

"August, why the fuck would you move to Florida?" Rory burst out, as if he'd been holding that in for far too long. Knowing him, he probably had. "What's waiting for you there?"

I scrubbed at my face. The truth, the one I knew deep down, was that I couldn't think of a good reason to go. "I'm just tired of being alone."

"Uh, pretty sure I'm right here," Rory said, pointing at his chest.

I shot him a look. "And you're going to renew our lease in six months and stay in this place forever and ever?"

"Well, fuck."

"Right." My chest sank at his frank answer, the reality settling in. It was one I'd been dealing with for a while now, as everyone made life plans that didn't include me. Sure, I might be a needy motherfucker, but I didn't think asking to be *someone's* priority was unreasonable.

"One question for you," he said. "And you can tell me to fuck off or not answer if you want."

"Shoot," I said, bracing myself for whatever truth bomb my best friend was about to drop.

"How's what your parents are doing with moving down to Florida any different from me moving out? What extra connection will you have there that you won't have here?"

Yup, gut punch. I chewed a few more mangoes to avoid answering, my chest throbbing with the truth that, yeah, even my folks had been focused on their relationship with the move, not their relationship with me.

Because they assumed I'd be off, making my own connections, settling down with someone on my own by now. Me fucking too.

"Hey, I'm not trying to be a dick here," Rory said, lifting his hands. "Just trying to point out that if you want to move, it needs to be because you want it. Not because you're afraid of everyone leaving you."

"Okay, you keep up like this, and I'll be KO'ed before we finish the conversation." Seriously, ouch. Rory was charging in here with a carving knife, and as much as I hated the lance of pain in my chest, all my avoidance hadn't forged any solutions either.

"What do you want?" Rory asked. "A life here, or a life somewhere else?"

Distilled like that, the answer was clear as daylight.

"Here."

The admission cracked open something in me, and the breath rushed out, as if I'd been socked in the stomach. From the moment my folks had announced they were moving, I'd been torn over the idea of not being able to drop by at any time. At the idea of them moving on without me.

But the truth was, I knew them. They'd visit me, and I'd visit them. There was no future where they'd disappear from my life. I'd just been paralyzed by the change, because everyone had found their connections, and I was stuck on the outside.

"Thank fuck," Rory said. "You looked miserable every time you mentioned Florida."

Relief flooded through me in a fierce, blinding torrent. Had the answer been that simple? I'd been tangled up with thoughts about this for weeks, but all it took was someone who knew me hammering a little bit of sense. No part of me had wanted to leave. I liked my life here. I liked where I worked, my friend group, and everything about the area.

The hard part would be telling my parents.

The other hard part would be pursuing what I really wanted.

Who I wanted.

Rory kicked me in the shin. "You haven't told me more about fire-fighter hottie either, though Nyx told me he's gorgeous. How come she and Owen got to meet him and not me?"

"Because he happened to be the one who answered the call over our fire alarm," I said, popping a few more pieces of mango. "Owen's still mortified over that one."

"And we'll never let Daddy Owen live that one down."

"How does Wyatt react to you calling another man Daddy?" I asked.

"Eye roll usually. He knows me," Rory responded. "Plus, it's not like he wants me calling him Daddy. Weird enough that I'm friends with his daughter."

"How is Harps doing?"

She was one of our old piercers who'd left to become a vet tech. We saw her once in a while, but she wasn't around as much as she used to be. One of the shifts that had me shaken, because Alchemy Ink was my other family.

"Killing it in school, but she misses the crew," Rory said. "Once the semester ends and she can breathe, she's coming out to movie night again." He eyed me. "But don't think I missed the dodge. Fess up about Drake."

Well, there went that attempt. My skin prickled, but I sucked in a deep breath. "We haven't had a relationship talk, but he's my ex's brother, so I'm guessing there's some shaky territory."

"But you're doing sleepovers, babe," Rory said, pushing up to sit on the side of the kitchen counter, and he swung his legs back and forth, clearly getting out his excess energy. "When I was avoiding anything that resembled commitment, I didn't sleep over. That was a GTFO as fast as possible."

"Fuck, I want him so badly," I murmured as I scrubbed at my face. "He doesn't get scared away if I send a thousand rambling texts, and he fucks like a dream."

"So when's the wedding?" Rory teased, his eyes sparkling. "But seriously, if I can survive dating my friend's dad and the weirdness with that, I think you can overcome his sister being your ex. You and...Salamandastron? You guys were barely dating. I didn't even meet her."

Rory was too far to kick, so I lobbed a crumpled-up napkin at him. "Serena. And yeah, I hadn't met her family either. But what if Drake says it's not worth the risk? Then I'm back at square one, loveless and alone."

"August, my sweet baby child, you'll never be completely alone. Even if your parents move, even if I live with Wyatt, you have people who love you who'll never let those connections wither away. And I know even if you don't end up with Drake, you'd find another roommate, and you'd win them over with your easygoing charm. And now I'm a little jealous because they better not take my place."

A laugh burst from me, but Rory's words were a lifeline, and I clung to the reassurance he offered.

"No one could take your place," I responded. "No matter what changes."

Rory arched a brow. "Now turn that back around and take some of your own advice."

I wrinkled my nose. "Rude. I get the message, though. I'll talk to Drake and my folks soon."

My heart thrummed a little harder at the prospect. While my folks might be disappointed, they'd love me no matter what I chose.

Drake, on the other hand....

In the short time I'd known him, I'd gotten deeply attached. Each hangout, sleepover, date, just brought us even closer. I couldn't imagine losing what we'd found.

But only the truth would tell if we would last.

Chapter Eighteen

Drake

"How're things coming with the fundraiser?" Chief Mahoney strolled into the kitchen.

Enthusiasm thrummed through me. Spring Fires was signed on, and Ethan seemed just as excited as I was for the event. I'd started coordinating ticket sales, and we'd be using the firehouse grounds for the show itself.

"So good," I said. "And you're sure the date works?"

"Yeah, I cleared it out," Chief said with a grin. He clapped me on the shoulder. "You're doing good, Drake. I can't wait to see how this turns out."

Warmth flowed through me. Even though I might always feel second-best with my family, here, I thrived. That was proof positive I was in the right place.

Just like the feelings August inspired in me were proving he was the right one.

I only needed to tell him.

"These guys are talented, and they're excited to help out the firehouse."

Ethan had mentioned he had a personal reason to, but he hadn't elaborated on it. I was just relieved August had made the initial connection. Who knew if my message would've gotten looked over otherwise?

"Considering the amount the guys are already discussing, I think it's fair to say you've got the younger folks interested, which was my hope." Chief leaned back against the counter. "Quiet day here?"

I was halfway through a twenty-four, and we'd barely heard a murmur, which was pretty normal for a Tuesday. In a small town like Kennett, we weren't facing a huge amount of constant fire crises. While working in a more high-profile area would be interesting, I enjoyed the peace and downtime too much to want to move.

When I imagined a future with August, which had been happening more frequently as of late, the pace of my job worked well for our life together. Which was fucking insane that I was even going down that train of thought.

I was so far gone on him, but I'd been too chickenshit to say anything on our date.

And I was even more chickenshit when it came to Serena.

The fire alarm bell began to ring.

"Spoke too soon," Chief said, striding in the direction of the PPE room. "Let's go get our turnout gear on."

"You coming out on this one, old man?" I teased, keeping pace with him.

Dooley rushed into the PPE room around the same time we did, but his pale face offered all the signal I needed.

"How bad?" I asked, heading to my locker. I started to strip down at once, the motions automatic as I ditched my clothes in the locker and tugged on my uniform and the turnout gear.

"Big fire over at Turnpoint Apartments," he said.

"Oh shit," I murmured. Apartment fires spread fast, and the individual destruction they caused was heartbreaking.

"I'll get a few more on the scene," Chief said, somehow already dressed in his turnout gear. "Dooley, you drive."

"Yes, sir," he said with a salute as he tugged on his own gear. We'd want every precaution for a fire like this.

My heart slammed hard as adrenaline coursed through my veins. Turnpoint Apartments was right on the edge of town, but it was a crowded complex, full of people who'd be in danger right now. We had to get to them.

"Let's head out," Dooley said, leading the way to the truck we'd be taking.

When I stepped into the garage with the truck, Chief strode in from the other side.

"Hannigan and Jacobs are already heading in. Let's take the Hazmat truck," he said. "I've got a bad feeling about this one."

My skin prickled with awareness. Chief's feelings were rarely wrong, and we'd learned to trust them over the years. "Noted."

Dooley pivoted to the other truck in the station, one equipped with materials to handle Class B and C fires. Fuck, those were always more of a challenge. The turnout gear was heavy but a familiar comfort, and I stepped into the back of the truck and found my spot, Chief taking the other side.

"We going now?" Dooley called back.

"Head off," Chief called. "Jacobs and Hannigan will be behind us."

With that, the bay doors opened, the engine rumbled, and the sirens began to ring.

We rushed out of the station and onto the street with a fluidity of motion I was used to, cars veering out of the way as we careened past streetlights and through the main stretch of town. Turnpoint Apartments was only minutes away from the firehouse, but when a fire was spreading through a huge place like that, every second counted.

And every second stretched longer and longer as we raced from one street to another en route.

Fuck, I wanted to let August know.

The fact he lingered on my mind even now solidified my feelings for him. Normally, on bigger calls, my thoughts flashed to my folks, my sisters, but they were circling around the one man who'd managed to work his way into my heart.

Who was all bright smiles, goofy jokes, and golden retriever energy I hadn't been able to stay away from.

The chief was quiet too, clearly wrapped up in his mind. He'd told me his thoughts always went to his wife and kids during these calls. I'd always been jealous of everything he'd built, how he'd managed to find himself something lasting even with the unpredictability and danger of the job.

For the first time, I had that hope too.

I just needed to tell August.

"Approaching," Dooley called out as we made a hard turn. I clutched the bar a little tighter. Who knew what we'd walk into? It could be a small apartment fire, but these weren't old, sturdy buildings—with some of the newer complexes, the shoddy materials lit up far too easily. My stomach roiled, unease spreading through me.

"Fuck," Dooley swore, and that confirmed it.

I met the chief's gaze, and the seriousness there etched into me. Readiness coursed through my system, one bred into me from countless fire calls, easy to difficult.

The truck came to a halt, and Chief and I jumped out from the side.

The blaze in front of us was bad.

Flames licked up the right side of the building, and Chief started to walk forward, doing his assessment of the area. Dooley and I rushed to grab the double jacket hoses, as well as the foam hose, and we got them prepared.

Chief jogged back over to us. "Looks like a class B fire based on the flames and spread. Start at it with the foam."

Already, crowds of people gathered out in the parking lot, huddled in groups of families, neighbors, as everyone stared on in horror. This sort of place, the fire could spread at a lightning pace, and everyone's homes were in danger. My mind zeroed in on assessing the damage that was visible.

"Anyone still inside?" I asked the chief.

He was already in motion, helping me and Dooley prep the foam hose, and we unrolled it at rapid speed, drawing it over in the direction of the blaze. The creak and groan and crackle of the flames were audible, even over the chatter from the crowd outside.

"Go check with the crowds," Chief directed, and I stepped away at once.

I jogged over to the first cluster of tenants. "Everyone get out okay?"

A woman raced up to me, tears running down her face. "My mother, she's trapped in there. She can't walk."

Oh, fuck.

"What part of the building?" I asked.

The woman pointed to the middle of the complex. The left side was fiercely burning, closing in on where she'd pointed. She'd be in imminent danger.

"Apartment 2b, on the second floor," she said, wringing her hands. "I drove over here when I heard about the fire."

My stomach bottomed out, but I radioed the chief. "Going in—middle section. Older woman trapped."

"Roger," Chief fired back.

With that, I took off.

My heart thumped hard in my ears as I secured all my gear and strode up to the central entrance. The door was locked, one of those that needed a passcode to get in, and metal at that. The window next to it was the easier entry point. I brought out my hatchet and began to hack away, the shattering of glass barely making a dent in the nearby roar of the fire. Already, stepping this close to the building brought the waves of smoke my way, the heat rising by the second.

Once I got the window cleared, I reached for the radio. "Entering now."

When I stepped inside, someone's bedroom greeted me, piles of dirty laundry and teetering stacks of books, but I strode through the apartment with ease. Once I emerged into the hallway, I headed in the direction of the stairwell. If the mother was on the second floor, I should be able to get to her quickly.

I marched down the main hall at an even speed, making sure to watch where I walked for any obstacles, as well as any glimmers of flame or plumes of smoke. I checked each room as I went, the doors still open, alert for any sounds of a person or animal who might've gotten left behind in the shuffle.

Farther down the hall, the flames were creeping forward, licking through apartment after apartment at an alarming speed. Given the builder, I wasn't surprised. Geraldo Building was notorious for using shit materials and not keeping everything to code, even as he churned out more new complexes every year.

I reached the stairs and thumped my way up, my heart rate accelerated.

The roiling smoke that had begun to crawl through the place was likely hazardous, and I was grateful for the SCBA gear I was breathing through. Especially if this had been caused by a gas leak or any other sort of class B situation. My body hummed with readiness, the way it always did during one of the more dangerous fires.

In these moments, I thrived. My adrenaline pumped, my body hummed with awareness, and I moved with an unparalleled deftness.

And yet, a new concern blossomed in the mix. If something happened to me here, I'd regret not saying anything to August.

I reached the second floor, and smoke crawled farther into the building, making visibility murkier. I checked the first door—apartment 2a. Chances were, the woman who was trapped would be close to here.

The door on the opposite side showed the exact one I searched for. I opened the door, which thankfully wasn't locked.

"Anyone in here?" I called out.

"Here," an older woman cried, coming from farther inside the apartment.

I rushed in the direction of the rooms, and in the middle of the hall, an older woman crawled forward, using her arms to propel her. My chest squeezed tight. Shit, had her relative not been outside, she never would've made it out on her own.

"Let's get you on my back," I said. "Trouble with the legs?"

"Yes," she gasped, sweat in a sheen across her forehead. I crouched down and helped her onto my back. Thankfully, she wasn't very heavy.

I gripped her arms to keep her in place, her legs too weak to brace herself on my back. Time to get the fuck out of here.

I headed out of her apartment again, this time with her on my back. When I reached the door, I stopped.

The fire had spread.

The stairwell I'd come up was swallowed in orange-gold flames, increasing by the second.

Fuck.

Looks like my luck had run out.

The roar of the fire was growing, those flames threatening top-speed decimation, and my heart sank.

My biggest regret was never telling August I loved him.

Chapter Nineteen

August

I worked on the watercolor in my stall, watching the vivid colors appear on the page. The sunset from my date with Drake remained in the forefront of my mind. My client load was lighter tonight due to a cancellation. Technically, I could cut out, but I liked taking the time to work in my space around people. Something comforting existed here that I treasured.

My earlier conversation with Drake was unfinished, but considering he was on a twenty-four, chances were he was dealing with business. He got a lot of random calls out, but I'd started to recognize the patterns. If I knew he was on a shift, his silence would be because of work. It was a reassurance compared to other partners where they'd ghost me or leave me on read.

He always managed to message back when he could, offering me a reassurance I hadn't realized I'd needed.

Everything with Drake was better than I could've imagined.

I wanted to keep him so badly.

And this time, I was going to try.

I snagged my phone and shot out a text. *Can you meet up anytime soon?*

I knew I wasn't going to get an immediate answer, but butterflies burst in my stomach. I'd tell him. He was worth the attempt.

"Shit. Shit, shit, shit." Rory burst into the back from where he'd been manning the front.

"What's wrong?" I shot up in my seat on instinct from the storm clouds broiling off Rory.

"I just saw a local alert—there's a bad fire at Turnpoint Apartments."

My heart stuttered and stilled.

Bad fire.

In the past, it was an abstract thing. The danger was sad but didn't strike as immediate. Right now, I connected the dots—because it was a local place, and that meant Drake was in the heart of the blaze.

No wonder he wasn't responding.

Fuck, what sort of bad was this fire? My brain spiraled to worst-case scenarios, and my stomach bottomed out.

"You okay?" Rory asked, concern clear in his eyes. It was obvious why he'd rushed back to tell me the news. "Why don't you get out of here? You don't have anything else on the books."

"Yeah," I said woodenly, my head bobbing with the nod. "Yeah, I'll do that."

Rory rested a hand on my shoulder. "He's a professional. He's done this before, and he'll make it through this too."

Even though his words were meant to be a comfort, my terror didn't subside. I hadn't ever experienced this kind of fear before, someone I'd fallen for in direct danger like this.

And if he made it out, if he wanted to pursue something with me, I'd experience this in the future again.

I swallowed hard, a metallic fear lingering on my tongue. Yet, I wanted him anyway. I couldn't turn off the feelings that erupted for him as much as I could stop breathing. If being with him meant worrying more or spiraling every now and again, he was worth it.

"You going to get out there or stare into space?" Rory said, his voice light.

"Right." I nodded, balled my hands into fists, and then shook them out.

"Going to the apartments would be the best chance of seeing what's going on."

Rory wasn't wrong. I just wasn't sure if I was ready for what I'd see when I got there. Still, I couldn't hang back. Not when Drake was out there and in danger, so close to me. My whole body was a taut string that could snap at any moment.

"I'll text you," I promised as I cleaned my brushes and put away my paints and the piece I was working on. That could be dealt with later.

"You'd better," Rory called as he walked toward the waiting area again. I patted my pockets down for my keys and wallet, then headed for the door. Rory offered a nod as I passed by, one I returned before stepping outside.

The sun was bright, but it didn't seep past my skin, not while my mind rioted. My legs grew numb as I quick-walked over to my car, barely able to register anything else. Fuck, what if Drake got trapped in the building? What if he got hurt?

This was something he did every day. Something he prepared for.

He had to make it out of this.

Because I needed to tell him that somehow, he'd become the person I thought of first when I woke up, and the one I lingered on when falling asleep. His presence dominated my attention, and being with him made hope blossom that those dreams of finding the right one for me might actually be fulfilled.

I turned on the ignition and set off down the street, clutching the steering wheel with enough force to take it off.

How bad was this fire? All I could see in my mind's eye was the decimated hulk of a shopping center that had been ravaged by a fire when I was little. I'd seen the scorched beams, the guts that remained of what used to be a bustling strip, but the fire had destroyed it.

Imagining someone surviving that. Fuck.

Black smoke billowed into the air as I neared the apartments.

My stomach churned. That couldn't be a good sign.

Sirens lit the air as I veered toward the apartment complex. Cops had arrived on the scene to help manage the crowds. I parked along the street instead of trying to get near the blockades already in place. Two fire trucks were stationed in the parking lot, and the glimmer of orange flames mingled with the plumes of choking black smoke that threatened to snuff out the horizon.

My heart accelerated as I parked and burst out of my car. The stench of the smoke was strong even here, adding to the churning in my stomach, and I loped up the grassy knoll leading to the parking lot for the apartment complex. The area by the road was being monitored by the cops, but I dodged in through the tree line, sneaking through.

The tenants were all clustered in groups across the parking lot, everyone giving the firefighters a wide berth. A woman was collapsed on the ground in tears with a few people surrounding her and trying to pat her on the back.

My heart squeezed tight. The crackle and groan of the timber sent bursts of panic through my system. Fuck. Where was Drake?

Two of the guys in turnout gear stood by the hose, sending volleys of foam to suppress the fire in the worst area.

Another of the guys raised the ladder to the second floor, and my heart snagged in my chest. Something deep in my gut told me Drake was in there. That he wasn't any of the guys out here.

And that gut instinct was one I didn't always listen to, even though it was always right.

The ladder stopped right by an open second-floor window. A minute later, a firefighter in turnout gear stepped up to it, someone hanging onto his back. He climbed onto the ladder with care and surety to his movements, a confidence I'd recognize anywhere.

Drake.

That had to be Drake.

Fuck.

He clutched the ladder, which began to slide back down, with him and an older woman on his back in tow.

"Oh my god!" A scream came from the crowd as the woman who'd been sobbing burst forward.

Another creak sounded, and part of the building behind them on the second floor crumbled. Just fucking fell away. My heart lodged in my throat. He'd been right there. So close to that.

Drake climbed off the ladder, carrying the elderly woman in the process, and got himself onto the ground.

Relief whooshed through me.

The cops were trying to keep the woman back, who attempted to rush Drake and the elderly lady. My hands balled into fists as I kept myself from bursting forward, just to see if Drake was okay. If he'd run into any trouble in there, incurred any wounds in the process.

I took a few steps closer, allowing myself that as he joined the others who were putting out the fire. Another hose added to the effort, and the foam began to suppress the sections it hit, similar to the way he'd smothered the one in my kitchen months ago—even though that felt like a lifetime now.

I swayed in place, relief pouring through me as more and more of the flames were doused, and the firefighters got them under control. Drake had gotten away from the building, which put him in less danger than he'd been in. The elderly lady was escorted to the woman who knew her, and they fiercely embraced. Pride thrummed in my chest.

Drake had done that.

He'd saved her life. Carried her out of danger.

As much as I was terrified for him, I was so achingly proud too.

I took a few steps closer, wanting to be near him with every fiber of my being. I wouldn't interfere while he was putting out the fire, but fuck, I needed to hold him, kiss him, be with him.

I wasn't sure how long I stood there and watched, but I remained steadfast as the crew handled putting out the fire. It went from a hearty blaze when I'd arrived to nothing but charred and smoking remains, covered in foam and then blasted by water.

My heart ached for the people affected by this fire—their homes, their possessions were all scorched to ash by the blaze. But after seeing the risk of more, that they could've gotten caught in there, I was relieved that all of them had escaped with their lives intact.

At long last, the fire crew stopped the spray of the hoses and began to tuck them away.

My feet carried me forward.

A shout sounded by my side, one of the cops signaling that I stand back, so I stilled where I was.

One of the firefighters looked in my direction, and he began striding my way.

Drake took off his helmet and mask, his sweat-soaked features dosing me with relief, longing, lust. Everything all at once.

A bright grin lit his face, one that pierced right through my heart. His expression held a giddiness that told me how much he loved this work, that he faced the danger gladly.

And I loved him a little more for it.

Drake walked over to me with long, loping strides, those muscular legs eating up the pavement. The cop seemed to relax once he saw Drake handling the situation and returned to helping situate the crowd.

"Heard there was a bad fire here," I said, my voice a little hoarse from watching in worried silence this whole time.

"Think we got it managed." He winked and slipped up to me. The space between us grew so tense I was surprised it didn't cause a spark on its own.

We hadn't proclaimed anything between us, and he stared at me, a searching in his eyes as if he was trying to figure out where we were too.

Fuck it.

I closed the space between us and pressed my lips to his.

He wrapped his hand around my nape, drawing me in as he hungrily met my kiss. Drake took control at once, his tongue driving into my mouth with a possessiveness that made me reel. After the fear that had roiled through me, kissing him filled me with such elation. My entire body burst with bright bubbles as I savored each kiss, each brush of our lips together.

God, this man was everything.

The stench of the smoke didn't even faze me as I drank in his presence, his commanding kiss. I loved him with my whole heart and soul, and I needed to tell him.

Whistles broke out from behind us, and Drake separated from me.

"Going to join the rest of us?" Dooley called over, a shit-eating grin on his face.

Drake lifted a hand. "Be right over." He shook his head, his dark eyes dancing. "I've got to get back to the job."

"Come to my place after?" I asked. "I'll leave a key under the door-mat."

Drake's eyes crinkled with his smile. "Fuck yes. That sounds per-fect."

He gave my nape one more squeeze before separating from me and then waved as he jogged over to the rest of his coworkers—who now knew something was going on between us.

I'd been nervous before, but the fact he'd publicly claimed me like that gave me hope that he wanted more too.

I brushed my fingers against my lips, still sensitive from those bruis-ing kisses, then headed off in the direction of my car.

Tonight, I'd make this real.

Chapter Twenty

Drake

The rest of my shift passed in a blur, including a hefty dosage of relentless ribbing from my coworkers.

I didn't give a fuck.

Claiming August in front of everyone felt damned right, and it only stoked the hope that he'd want a relationship too. And once we got a second to breathe, we'd have a talk. *The* talk.

I managed to finish my shift and drove to August's house, which I hadn't been to since we'd first met. When I'd burst in to put out a kitchen fire.

My heart thudded hard as I approached the front door and reached under the mat to find the promised key. I knew he had a roommate, but we hadn't met. Hopefully he'd let him know I was coming over.

Granted, it was three in the morning, which was an awkward time to visit. I'd finished a little later than planned due to cleanup from the apartment fire.

I padded through the house, feeling like an interloper. The shadows stretched, scraps of moonlight from the windows the only light in the main room. I meandered toward a light coming from farther down the hall, trying not to stomp too loudly, even though my boots were heavy. One of the bedroom doors lay open, and I peered inside to see August passed out in the bed, the moonlight spilling over his features. The sight made my heart speed up. No one had ever made me feel like this, as if I was coming home.

Which was why I needed to find a way to keep him.

I stripped out of my boots, my pants, and my shirt, leaving me in just my boxer briefs as I stepped into the bed with a creak. He rustled, those sleepy eyes blinking open.

"Drake?"

"It's still okay that I'm here, right?" I asked, wanting to double check.

"More than," he said, patting the bed beside him. "C'mere."

I slipped under the covers beside him, and his arms wrapped around me at once. When I glanced over, his eyes had already shut again, and his breaths were evening. I settled against the pillow, taking comfort in the warmth of his body, in his smooth skin, his regular breaths puffing against me.

I was out within minutes.

***

When I woke up, the sun was streaming through the blinds. The bright red numbers on the clock read ten in the morning, which meant I had caught some solid sleep. Hadn't been hard with August by my side. I'd never slept so well.

Voices sounded from the other room, so I slipped on my pants and padded out of the bedroom.

August sat at the kitchen table while another guy perched on the counter.

When August's gaze landed on me, he lit up with a smile that overtook his features. My heart skipped a beat.

A whistle sounded, and the guy hopped off the counter. "Rory," he said. "I finally get to meet hottie firefighter."

"Back off," August grumbled. "You've got Wyatt."

Amusement fluttered in my chest, and I offered a nod. "Drake, though I prefer hottie firefighter." I closed the distance between me and August, and I dipped down to press a kiss to his lips. August melted into me at once, and I lingered there for a moment, enjoying the public claiming.

When I pulled back, Rory was watching us intently. He fit the tattoo shop vibe, dark hair, gauges, and covered in tattoos. He was a slender twink with a glint in his eyes, who looked like nothing but trouble, and I could see at once why he and August got along—complete opposites.

"I approve," Rory said. "I'd give you the don't hurt him speech, but you're both consenting adults and can figure out your own shit." He snagged his keys with a jangle. "With that, I'm off to let you fuck like bunnies."

August opened his mouth in protest, and I placed my finger over his lips.

"Thanks." I winked back, and Rory let out a bark of a laugh.

"This one's a keeper, Auggie," he called back as he headed for the door.

The second it shut with a click, I sank into the seat beside August. "As much as I want to fuck your brains out right now, I think we need to talk first."

He straightened in his seat, his eyes growing wide.

"Nothing bad, I swear," I said, lifting my hands. "In fact, the opposite of bad, I hope."

"I'minlovewithyou," August blurted out.

"Wait, what?" My brain tried to parse the words, not daring to hope they were what I thought I'd heard.

His cheeks reddened, and he ducked his head. "I'm in love with you."

Butterflies erupted inside me, giddiness lifting me up like champagne bubbles. I tilted his chin up so his eyes met mine. "Well, then, lucky me. Because I'm in love with you too."

"No shit?" He tilted his head to the side, those hazel eyes widening.

A laugh burst out of me. Fuck, he was so cute. "Yeah, baby. In case it wasn't completely obvious, I'm gone on you. I thought relationships were too difficult to bother with. That no one would be able to deal with me as-is, and you swept in and proved me wrong. Everything with you is easy in a way I'm not used to. You just get me like no one else has managed to."

"Are you sure I'm not too needy?" August asked. "It's been an issue before."

I stroked my thumb over his lower lip, and he let out a puff of air.

"Nah. You're perfect for me. I didn't realize how much I was missing out on until I met you."

He swallowed hard and leaned in to press his lips against mine. I savored the kiss, the sweetness that trickled through me like honey. I wove my fingers through his hair, loving the way he responded, how he melted for me. I climbed onto his lap, straddling him as I kissed the hell out of my man. I loved that we were so close in size, that I could perch here without breaking him.

He wrapped his hands around my waist and returned every kiss with a ferocity that promised he meant everything he'd said.

When we broke for breath, the smile he gave me was radiant.

"So does that mean you're my boyfriend?" he asked, chewing on his spit-slicked lower lip.

"Hell yes," I said, pecking another quick kiss on his lips. Euphoria burst through me, and I couldn't bother containing it.

He wrinkled his nose. "What are we going to tell your sister?"

I sucked in a breath. This was what I'd struggled with the entire time I'd been attracted to August and quickly falling, but I'd come to terms with it at last. "That you're mine. Serena's reasonable to a fault—if anyone could handle this news, it'd be her."

"You're not wrong there," August said with a grin. "I think our breakup was the most chill thing from her end."

"Yeah, that wouldn't fucking happen with me," I growled. "You're not going anywhere, get that?"

He beamed back at me. "God, you're everything I've ever wanted."

Those words sank right into the core of me. All the times I'd never felt like enough, second rate, the backup option.

But August treated me like a first choice. Like I mattered to him as much as he mattered to me. And damn, I was obsessed.

"Same," I admitted, brushing my thumb against his pretty lower lip again. "I'm so fucking glad Serena sent me over here to bring your stuff back."

"Well, if you hadn't, who would've saved me from my kitchen fire?" he teased. "Though, as terrifying as yesterday was, you looked hot as fuck."

"Given the amount of fire, yeah," I said back, amusement bubbling in me.

He pinched me in the side. "Fine, you're sexy as fuck."

"Well, so are you," I responded, trailing my fingers over his clavicle, along his side. He was all slim muscle, tattoos, and a bright smile I couldn't get enough of. "Goddamn, I want to sink inside you. There was a moment yesterday when the stairwell caught fire and I had to reroute, and I wasn't sure I'd make it back. All I could think about was you."

August's eyes took on a watery sheen, and he sucked in a sharp breath. "I was so fucking scared when I heard about the apartment fire. But I get why you do it. Why you need to. And I'll be there to support you however you need it."

If I wasn't already sitting, I'd be knocked out at the knees.

My chest squeezed tight, acceptance hitting me square there. I hadn't realized how badly I'd longed to hear that.

"I'm going to defile you now," I murmured, nipping his ear. "Any problem with that?"

"Oh hell no," he said, those gorgeous eyes gleaming. "I want that cock lodged in my throat, my ass, any way you can take me."

"Fuck," I growled, sliding off his legs to stand. In a quick movement, I scooped him up off the chair and carried him toward the bedroom. "I'm going to fuck you until you're screaming my name."

Chapter Twenty-One

August

"**I** got my test results," I blurted out, the moment he swept into the room with me in his arms.

His eyes widened. "And?"

"Negative," I said, a little breathless with the possibilities. "So if you want to..."

"Damn, baby," he murmured. "That changes my plans completely."

"That a bad thing?" I asked, chewing on my lower lip. Based on the blaze in his eyes, the switch-up might be even better.

"Hell no," he responded, dropping me down on my mattress. "I have an important question though. Do you have any plugs or prostate massagers?"

"Fuck yes," I said, spreading my legs in invitation. "Bottom drawer of my nightstand. Lube's there too."

The wicked grin on Drake's lips scorched me through.

We were dating now.

He fucking *loved* me.

The craziest thing was that for the first time, I didn't feel like I was the odd man out. Like I was too much or gunning in too hard because he matched me every step of the way.

"Strip for me," he said as he crouched in front of my nightstand, rummaging through my collection. "Someone's a slut for getting filled, isn't he?"

Ngh. That mouth.

I tugged my tee off and ditched the sweats. I hadn't bothered with underwear because yes, I had absolutely expected to get laid. The need had grown so strong I was prepared to beg for his cock. Whenever he ever wanted mine, I was happy to deliver—I didn't hate topping or anything—but my preference had always been bottoming, and not all of my partners wanted to top me.

Drake seemed happy to steer this ship.

I lay on the bed bare ass naked and spread my legs, ready to accept whatever he wanted to give me.

Drake stood again and kicked off his sweats, which showcased those rock-hard thighs, his thick, veined cock with the darker mushroom head that I sorely wanted in my mouth and in my hole. Pre-cum beaded on his tip, the slight glisten there beckoning me.

"Damn, you need some breakfast, baby?" he teased, his eyes dancing.

I nodded. "Yes. Now."

Drake's smile was deadly and gorgeous, knocking the breath from me. I had a hard time believing he was all mine. And yet, he settled between my thighs and squeezed lube onto his fingertips, slicking up a large vibrating plug of mine. Fuck yes. He didn't bother prepping me beforehand, aware by now what a slutty hole I had. Instead, Drake eased the plug inside me. The stretch and slight burn was perfect, and a moan escaped me. He tapped the vibration on at the end, and pleasure flooded through me at once.

"Now that one of your needy holes is filled, let me take care of your mouth," he said, prowling up my body. My cock brushed against the hard muscle, and damn, a shiver rippled through me. Drake straddled me, his thick thighs bracketing my shoulders, and the tip of his cock hovered right in front of my mouth.

Goddamn. The scent of him, the slightly smoky cedar, enraptured me, and I opened my mouth at once, ready to suck him down. With the vibration in my hole, I was beyond turned on, my cock hard and dripping, my body sensitized.

He circled his hand around the base of his cock and brushed his tip across my lower lip. I licked at it to taste the salt of his pre-cum.

"Damn, good boy," he said. "Want to choke on it, baby?"

I whimpered as he thrust the tip of his cock into my mouth. I sucked on reflex, and a moan erupted from me at the weight of it on my tongue, the flavor exploding in my mouth. Drake began to shift his hips, feeding his cock to me inch by inch. I continued to swallow more and more of it, the heaviness there, the velvet feel already making me float. God, I could suck his dick all day. And with my hole stuffed up, pleasure thrummed through my entire body.

He speared his fingers through my hair, a slight sting with the motion, and my lashes fluttered. The heat of being bracketed by his body, his thighs on either side of me, sent me into overdrive. I'd clearly died and gone to heaven. He thrust his cock into my mouth, and I choked as it started to glide down my throat.

"Fuck, the sounds you make," he purred. "So damn sexy. Love the way you choke on my cock."

God. This man. My eyes rolled back, heat rushing through me in a fierce sweep at his low, seductive voice. I could come just from his dirty talk. My balls twitched, heavy and full from the waves of pleasure the vibrating plug kept flooding me with, but I didn't want to come until he was fucking me.

He began to thrust deep down my throat, his balls smacking against my chin. Drool dribbled from my mouth, some of it trickling down my neck. I breathed through my nose, my throat stuffed full, my ass full and humming, and the overload was everything I could've hoped for. I loved how well he understood me, how I didn't even need to communicate some of the desires I'd held.

Instead, he filled me up and took over, and my mind blissed out in response. The stinging tug on my hair, the stretch of my lips, the heavy weight of his length on my tongue, everything turned me on more and more.

"Holy shit, your mouth is so hot," he groaned, fucking into me with a finesse that had me drooling more and more. "So fucking good."

The heat from him surrounding me caused sweat to prickle across my forehead, each breath through my nostrils feverish as he fucked my mouth like he owned it. In a way, he did. I surrendered to him completely, my eyes fluttering shut, allowing those sensations to wash through me. My balls ached, my cock leaked, and I was a ball of coiled need with the way the vibrations kept my prostate on edge, but I didn't want to stop sucking on him either.

"God, your sweet mouth is going to make me come," he moaned as he thrust in again.

A muffled groan came from me as his balls slapped against my chin again.

"Except I have plans for that load, and it's not in your mouth," he growled. He tugged at my hair and slowly pulled back. I surged forward, chasing his cock, but he yanked hard at my hair to keep me in place. "Nuh uh, baby."

He withdrew his cock, and I gasped in noisy breaths. My throat was a little raw from the pounding it had taken, and yet I craved more.

"Fuck, those lips are so glossy," he said, reaching down and rubbing his thumb across the spit-slick there. "So messy."

He wasn't wrong. I wiped my forearm across my mouth, ridding myself of some of the drool that had pooled there.

"Let me sink into that sweet hole," he said. "I can't wait to fill you up with my cum."

Fire roared through me at those words. Fuck, I hadn't been bare with a partner before unless they'd been pegging me, but getting flooded with cum was something I'd fantasized about for years.

Drake pushed up, then slid down my body until he kneeled between my spread legs. I widened them, as if I could make it clearer exactly where I wanted him. A winsome grin lit his face as our eyes met, and the tenderness there sent a vicious streak of joy through me. This man was mine.

He tapped at the base of the plug, which sent a jolt through me. My breath hitched, and his wicked eyes danced.

"You're so responsive," he said. "It's a dream."

"I'll be even more responsive when you get your cock back inside me," I promised.

His grin sharpened, and he tugged at the plug. He slowly drew it out of me, and I bit my lower lip to restrain my pout, because what he'd be replacing it with would be so much better. After being so full of his cock and the plug though, I craved something again in a fierce way.

Drake reached to the side to snag the lube, and he slicked his cock up. "God, your hole's so pretty. It's going to feel so damn amazing."

I swallowed hard. "I want you."

His expression softened. "You've got me, baby. All of me."

The seriousness in his tone burrowed right through me. This was more than just a heat of the moment fuck. No, I loved this man. Somehow, he'd snuck his way into my heart without even trying, and I didn't want to be extricated—ever.

He brushed his tip against my hole, and the shock of skin to skin there rippled through me. Pure electricity. Every damn time. I grabbed the back of my thighs and spread myself wide, desperate to have him deep inside me.

"Fuck me."

"Damn straight," he said as he thrust in a few inches. I barely noticed the stretch after having the thick plug inside me, but the glide—fuck, I'd never felt anything so good. Having him in me bare was beyond my wildest dreams, and he lived up to every single one.

"Holy shit," he groaned.

"Yeah," I gasped as he sank in further. The moment he settled fully inside me, the fullness solidified something inside me that I hadn't realized I'd craved. The thickness of his length, the way he connected with me in a way no one ever had before—on multiple levels—and how I was so far gone in love with him. He gripped my thighs tight, and I let go.

Drake drew back and thrust deep inside me again. The breath flew out of me as pleasure slammed into me hard.

"Oh god." My body would be a trembling mess in no time.

He tilted his head back, showing off the strong lines of his neck. "Fuck, I'm going to have to take my sweet time with you, baby. Otherwise I'll blow my load too fast."

A whimper escaped me.

He eased back in, nice and slow, the glide excruciating. Sweat burst on my forehead, my arms, my chest. My cock dripped, my balls ached, and the moans poured out of me as he brushed along my prostate. Fireworks flared fast and fierce. God, he felt so damn sinful. I was addicted to the heat of him, the thickness of his cock, the way the skin-to-skin connection elevated everything between us a thousand-fold.

"You," he purred as he thrust in slow. "You are all I've ever wanted."

His words took root deep in my chest, ones I'd been longing to hear after year and year of striking out in relationships. Fuck. I loved him so damn much, and I couldn't believe we were together. That we'd somehow crashed into each other's lives at the perfect time.

He fucked in again, a long, low groan rumbling from him. The glide against my prostate was excruciating, yet I didn't want the pleasure to end at the same time.

"Fuck, fuck, fuck," I gasped. The scent of sweat was heavy in the air, thick with lust from the sheer tension between us. Drake gripped my legs tightly as he thrust over and over, each stroke slow and simmering, each one bringing me closer and closer to implosion. I memorized his features—the sweat-soaked, dark strands of hair swaying with each movement, his deep brown eyes and long lashes, and his broad shoulders, defined muscles, that emanated such immense power.

I needed his cock in me like I needed my next breath, but the steady, increasing tension rose inside, the urge to come rolling in fierce and fast.

"Goddamn, baby," he groaned as he sank in again. "You feel so good bare."

I never wanted to go back. Just wanted him to take me like this day in and out. The increase of sensation, how his velvet heat felt gliding inside me—damn, it was incomparable. He dragged his cock along my prostate again, and I moaned loud and long, my head tipping back. My hole was stuffed full in a way I craved, and with Drake clutching my legs, ramming into me and bringing me to ecstasy over and over, I longed to stay like this forever.

I began to shift my hips onto his cock, chasing the sensation every time he pulled away. My entire body hummed on the edge of explosion, the ache in my balls growing agonizing. I wasn't sure how much longer I could take.

Drake began to fuck in harder, faster, his breaths huffing out of him. Each stroke sent a burst of pleasure as he tagged my prostate over and over. My legs full-out shook at this point, my body a tense wire begging to be plucked. The smack of skin meeting skin echoed through the room, and I relished each sensation as they collided with each other, building into this beautiful crescendo that I barreled toward.

"Fuck, I'm going to come," he groaned, a raggedness in his tone that I felt. He wrapped his hand around my cock, and oh fuck. The contact was all I needed.

My balls drew up, and my orgasm flew from me like a gunshot. Cum splattered between us, drops making a mess, and my vision stuttered, the sheer intensity of the pleasure slamming into me like a sucker punch. Bliss raced through my bloodstream, and I sailed higher than I ever had before.

"Hngh." Drake gripped me tight, and a second later, he came, his muscles tightening at once. The warm gush of cum flooded my insides.

Euphoria burst through me. Fuck, I wanted him to leave load after load inside me, filling me up until I was dripping.

I reached up for his arm and rested my hand there. "Don't pull out," I murmured. "Please."

He carded his fingers through his hair, his breaths coming in ragged. "Wasn't planning on it." The lazy, sated smile disarmed me. My heart swooped at the sight of him looming over me, my hole full of his cum, his cock still lodged inside. I'd barely come down to earth from that life-changing orgasm, and instead I floated in this relaxed, comfortable space.

"Mmk, baby," he murmured as he shifted his cock inside me a little and adjusted until he was lying on the bed behind me, his length plugging me up. I chewed on my lower lip, a sinful thrill rising inside me. I didn't want him to pull out. "I've got you." His arm slung around me, and he squeezed me tight. His sticky chest plastered to my back, but I didn't give a damn. I wanted to feel him against me, surrounding me, inside me.

Like this, we were connected in a way I'd always dreamed of with a partner.

"Can I keep you?" I asked, heat rushing to my cheeks at the admission. "This isn't going to just be some elaborate prank?"

Drake pinched me in the thigh as he pressed a kiss to my neck. "Only if I can keep you. And I'm shit at pranks, anyway."

"You're aware when I go all in, I go all in," I mumbled, the things I'd kept pent up pouring out of me. Apparently, a dick in the ass was my new truth serum.

"Good," Drake said, his words muffled as he kept mouthing kisses over my neck, my shoulder. "I've never had a partner go all in when it came to me."

My heart squeezed tight. How could anyone not? Drake Castillo was utter perfection. "Well, then I hope you're ready for the onslaught."

"Can't fucking wait." He pressed another idle kiss to the back of my neck, his words growing slurred. A snore sounded from behind me a moment later.

A laugh burst out of me, but I settled against the pillow and closed my eyes. With him buried inside me, his arms wrapped around me, I'd never felt more complete.

Chapter Twenty-Two

Drake

S treams of sunlight poured in through the windows of Artificer Coffee.

I sat at the table off to the side, clutching my mug tight. August sat next to me, his foot thumping to the same nervous beat as my heart. He took the occasional sip of his tea but kept glancing at the window.

Today we were meeting up with Serena.

A few days had passed since we'd officially decided we were dating, and we'd been glued together every chance we got outside of our work shifts. I never thought I'd need or want that from a boyfriend, but August proved otherwise. Being around him was like soaking in a perfect summer day, all crisp skies, the slightest breeze, and sunshine in spades. I was thoroughly addicted.

But I also couldn't push off this conversation with my sister any longer.

"What if she's pissed?" August wrinkled his nose. "I haven't even told my parents that I'm not moving with them yet. Then I'll have multiple people pissed at me. I might disintegrate from the pressure."

A laugh exploded from me. "I doubt you'll disintegrate, even if people are mad at you."

He'd told me about how his parents had wanted him to move and how he'd been torn. The idea he'd almost slipped through my grasp made my heart speed up.

Thank fuck he wasn't going anywhere.

August was mine, and I'd prove that to him every damn day.

"It's five minutes before our meetup time, and she's not here," August said. "She's got to be pissed."

I snorted. He wasn't wrong that something was off. Serena was always punctual, and to her, punctual meant being places fifteen minutes early. I'd been so nervous about telling her, that the news would somehow fracture things between us, but after claiming August, I was ready to face the challenge head-on.

If I could get over her ruining my graduation party with a keg stand gone wrong, she could handle me dating her ex.

Maybe different categories there, but hey, I had to hold onto some hope.

I sipped at the cappuccino, soaking in the warmth of that and August's constantly vibrating leg, which brushed against mine over and over. It was causing so much friction I half expected it to catch fire. I leaned in so my lips rested against his ear. "Nervous? Need something to suck on?"

His breath hitched, which sent a thrill through me. Fuck, his mouth, his hole, I couldn't get enough of either, and apparently, he felt the same way about my cock. Match made in heaven. August's hazel eyes were blown, the slight flush on his cheeks telltale. Clearly, our minds were in the same gutter.

The door to Artificer swung open, dragging my attention away.

Serena strode inside, wearing a black suit jacket and slacks that made me feel out of place in my jeans and tee. Which was ridiculous, because there were more hipsters than business professionals in here, so I should've felt right at home.

Except I was about to break the news to my sister that I was dating her ex-boyfriend.

"August?" Serena asked, glancing between us.

My stomach sank. Okay, well, maybe I was a little more worried than I'd let on. I sucked in a sharp breath, ready to launch into explanation mode.

Serena clasped her hands together and let out a squeal, which was so unlike my sister I blinked.

"What?" I scratched at my nape, feeling like I was missing something.

She plunked into the seat we'd left for her and picked up the mocha I'd bought—her favorite. "This mine? I'm guessing you didn't drag me out here to tell me you guys have become best friends."

"We're dating," I admitted, her behavior still confusing the fuck out of me.

"And we understand if you're angry," August rushed in. "I know it's got to be a bit odd, considering, well…"

"What, the fact we dated?" Serena said. "No offense, but I'm not the relationship type. And even if I was, after a month or two, it felt more like dating my brother, which was just weird. But it did give me the idea."

"The idea for what?" I asked, even though the pieces were slotting together at a rapid pace.

"To get you two to meet," Serena said, arching her brow. "Why do you think I gave you my ticket?"

"Because you know I love the Dropkick Murphys and wanted to see that concert?" I said, even though based on her smug smile, I'd figured it out. Relief saturated through me in a fast sweep.

"Yeah, but we started dating, not just being friends," August insisted, a seriousness in his gaze that was utterly adorable.

"Baby, she was playing matchmaker," I said, reaching over to squeeze his hand. "She wanted us to date."

"Whoa, what?" August glanced between us. His brows rose an inch.

Serena let out a bark of a laugh. "My brother needs some sunshine in his life. You're easygoing enough that I knew you wouldn't have an issue with his work schedule like past boyfriends did, and you're both into the worst fucking music."

"No accounting for taste," I commented. "Rich, coming from someone who likes stoner jam bands."

"I want to unwind on my downtime, not get amped up with a bunch of sweaty assholes," Serena said, taking another sip from her mocha.

"You really don't care?" August asked, his leg slowing down from the nervous movement.

"I'm glad," she said. "You're a good person, and I think you'll be great for Drake. He's been lonely, even if he'd never admit it."

"I'm right here," I grumbled, even though affection bubbled up inside me. She wasn't wrong. Meeting August and falling for him had made me realize how much I'd given up on trying to find love. How much I'd walled myself off.

And how much I'd secretly craved someone to come home to. To call my own.

"I know you are, little brother," Serena said, reaching out to pinch my cheek. I swatted at her, and she swatted back, and the years melted away, as if we were still teens and not in our late twenties.

"Well, damn, that's a huge relief," August said as he rested his ankle over mine, as if he couldn't bear for us to not be connected skin to skin. I loved every second of his neediness, as it soothed the need to be first for someone that had hounded me my entire life. I hadn't realized until I'd started dating him just how much my past relationships had been lacking.

"Did you think I'd be mad?" Serena asked.

"Yeah, a little," I admitted. "I felt super guilty at first. You have to admit, it looks bad on paper."

"I broke up with August though," Serena pointed out. "We'd barely been dating."

"Six months isn't anything to scoff at," he said.

Serena shook her head, a grin on her lips. "I wasn't aware we were dating past the initial hookup. For like three of those months."

"My whole world is a lie." August flung an arm over his forehead, faking drama.

"You're going to hold this over me, aren't you." I eyed Serena suspiciously.

"Oh, fuck yeah," she said with a toothy grin. "When it's time to give speeches at your wedding, you best bet I'm taking *all* the credit."

Heat rushed through me at the thought. With anyone else, I would've run screaming or wouldn't believe it could last. August's eyes sparked at the mention of wedding, and my chest squeezed tight. Yeah, he was definitely it for me.

I didn't care that we hadn't been together long. I knew, deep in my gut, that he was my forever guy.

"That's a deal," I said, and Serena's eyes widened.

"Damn, when you go in, you go all in," she said.

"Me or him?" August asked.

Serena shook her head. "That could apply to either of you. So clearly you were made for each other."

I reached under the table and linked hands with him, our fingers intertwining. August's eyes met mine, a softness in his hazel gaze that struck right to the core of me. Goddamn, I was so fucking lucky.

"Ugh, are you both going to be gross like that?" Serena wrinkled her nose and took another sip of her mocha. "Love is nauseating."

"Okay, ice queen," I responded with an eye roll. Moments like these, I forgot what a wild success Serena was and we vaulted back to the way we were as kids.

"Are you going to the fundraiser?" August asked, and I squeezed his hand a little tighter.

"The whatnow?" Serena asked, drilling me with her "lawyer look."

"I hadn't mentioned it to the family yet," I murmured to August.

"Oh, shit." He slapped a hand over his mouth. "Forget I said any-thing."

Serena shook her head. "Nuh uh, you're not getting out of that. Either of you. What fundraiser?"

"Sorry" August mouthed at me, but I shook my head, a rueful grin on my lips. Not like I needed to keep the event from my family. I just had my own personal hangups.

"I'm in charge of the firehouse fundraiser coming up, and it's a show—Spring Fires as well as some other bands." My shoulders tensed.

"What the fuck, asshat?" Serena reached across the table and smacked me in the shoulder. "Why were you keeping that from us? Did you think we wouldn't support you?"

I shrugged, staring at the wood grain of the table. "It's not a huge deal or anything."

"Yeah it is," August said, his voice serious. "This is something you've worked really hard on pulling together. And I know how excited you are about it."

"Which is why you're going to tell the rest of our family, and we'll all be there," Serena said, giving me daggers. "Why do you get weird about shit like that?"

"It's... Shit, Ser, I'm not a success like you and Blair." I opened my mouth, but the words gummed there. August holding my hand was keeping me tethered in the moment though, his support something I hadn't realized how badly I needed.

"I want to reach over the table and smack you," Serena muttered. "There's no competition, you get that? Are you happy?"

"Yeah," I murmured, sneaking a glance to August, who beamed back at me.

"Then you're killing it. That's the only metric anyone in our family gives a damn about." She leaned forward and smacked me hard on the arm again. "Changed my mind. It was worth it."

"Thanks," I murmured, my throat growing tight. Shit, all this sappiness couldn't be good for me. "Ow, I feel like you bruised the arm."

"You're full of shit," Serena said, finishing off the dregs of her mocha. "While I would love to stay and chat, I've got another client meeting in fifteen. Send me the details about your fundraiser before the end of the night, or else." She rose from her seat, entering and exiting like a tornado. Serena glanced between the two of us again.

"Called it." Her eyes twinkled, and she strode off in the direction of the front door.

"What the hell just happened?" August blinked a few times.

"I mean, you dated her," I said. "You didn't expect this?"

"Uh, apparently I didn't know her that well," he scratched at his nape.

"Well, I'm glad for that, baby," I said, slipping my arm around his shoulders. "There's only one Castillo I want you falling for."

"Your other sister?" he teased.

I pinched him in the side, and he yelped. "Ass."

He leaned in against me, and I didn't even give a damn that we were being the PDA couple in the coffee shop. "I don't know if I've ever fallen this hard." He glanced up. "That scare you?"

"Not in the slightest," I said. "As long as you can handle my odd shifts, my weird needs to go adventuring at midnight once in a while, and that I'm never going to be polished."

August lifted up one of his tattooed arms. "What the fuck about this says polished? You're dating a tattoo artist, not a banker."

"Thank fuck." A giddy laugh exploded out of me, and I soaked in the bliss of the moment—August by my side and the reality that we were just at the beginning.

We had a whole future of adventures ahead of us to dive headfirst into, and I couldn't wait.

Chapter Twenty-Three

August

"**A**uggie, you've got a visitor," Nyx called from over at her booth. "Some hot firefighter come to hose you down."

I rolled my eyes. The crew at the shop had been relentless since I'd told them Drake and I were dating. I'd be a liar if I said I didn't love it though. Their nosiness was how they showed they cared, and I was incapable of being smothered. We'd gotten through the coffee meetup with Serena yesterday, but tonight was dinner with my folks, where I had to explain to them not only was I seeing someone, but I also wouldn't be heading down to Florida with them.

I'd been breaking out in nervous sweats all day.

Drake agreed to meet me here first and wait around while I finished two short appointments—the clients wanted a set of coordinates, which should be an easy in and out and wrapped up in a half hour.

Drake strode to the back with the confidence that drew my attention every time. I'd fallen asleep last night with his cock in my mouth, and when I woke up in the middle of the night, that ended with me swallowing another load before I'd snuggled back up against him and passed out again.

He wore an open short sleeve button-down with a black tee that hugged his lithe form as well as form-fitting jeans that showed off his thick thighs. Goddamn. I wanted to sink my teeth into all that muscle.

"You're drooling," Cas said, peeking out from his booth.

"For fuck's sake," I muttered, though I reached up to wipe it off—because I was.

Still, his dark hair was styled, his deep brown eyes shone with warmth, and his lips looked enticing as hell. My chest squeezed tight. And he was all mine. Giddiness erupted the way it continued to with the realization. I'd wanted someone by my side for so long, and Drake matched me in every way. Whether we were taking random drives at two in the morning on the highway, blasting punk music out of the stereo, or trying hikes in places we hadn't yet discovered, every moment with him offered an excitement I was hooked on.

I'd never grow tired of this man.

"C'mere, baby," he murmured as he offered a hand. I took it, and he hoisted me up and then yanked me forward. My chest collided with his, and he leaned down to claim my mouth in a searing kiss. I melted into it as the adrenaline hit my system, waking me up better than a shot of espresso. My whole body came to life in his presence, an undeniable awareness there that I'd recognized from the start.

A cough sounded from behind us. "Uh, August, your next clients are here." Owen's voice was close—had he brought them back?

I pulled away from Drake at once, my cheeks flushed. When I turned to face my boss, he stood beside two very familiar people.

"Mom? Dad?" My whole body torched into embarrassment. Shit, they'd seen me kissing Drake. Their eyes widened, and they stared between us. Owen's words crashed in, and my brows furrowed. "Wait, clients?"

Mom's eyes sparkled with her grin. "Yeah, your father and I wanted to surprise you. Looks like you had a surprise for us too."

"I'll leave you guys to it," Owen said, offering a wave. His mouth twitched in amusement. "The rest of you, get back to your booths."

Cas let out a huff but leaned back. Guaranteed he and Nyx would be listening in on everything we said.

"So, wait, is this an actual appointment?" I asked, still not putting everything together. "Or just a work visit?"

"An actual appointment," Dad said. "Mom and I figured we would try being brave enough to get tattoos of our own. We didn't expect this though." Dad paused to glance over at Drake, who'd shoved his hands into his pockets. "Boyfriend?"

"Yeah," he said, tugging a hand out and extending it. "Drake Castillo. Happy to meet you."

"Castillo..." Mom said, a thoughtful look flickering across her features.

I scrubbed at my face. Oh god, this would be embarrassing. "My ex-girlfriend's brother, yeah." While Serena might not have mentioned me to her family, I'd yammered at length to my folks about her, the way I did about everyone I dated. Well, everyone up until Drake, but that was because I'd been so tangled up in their move and confused about what he and I were.

Dad let out a whistle. "That going to be complicated?"

Drake shook his head with a laugh. "Nah, Serena's not the type to seriously date, but I am. And August is amazing."

My heart thumped hard, and I passed him a grateful look. The tenderness in his gaze caused butterflies to explode in my chest all over again.

"He is," Mom said. "I'm glad you see that." She placed a hand on my shoulder. "Now, can I get mine over with first because I'm terrified and ready to chicken out."

I shook my head, even though a grin spread on my lips. "I never expected the two of you to get tattooed."

"It's your art, sweetheart," Mom said. "Can you blame me for wanting to carry a little of that with me?"

My heart squeezed tight.

"I'll keep Drake here company," Dad said. "Do we wait out in the front? Or can we watch?"

"Go grab chairs," I said. "You can pull them up and watch if you want." I brought Mom over to the table, my palms sweatier than normal. While this was a garden-variety tattoo, just a few numbers and marks, I hadn't expected to be tattooing my parents. And I still hadn't broken the bad news to them—that I wouldn't be moving. "And you," I gestured to Mom. "You sit here."

"When did you two start dating?" Mom asked while I bustled around, preparing all the equipment. The motions came automatically, which was good because my brain had checked the fuck out.

"I'm so sorry but I can't move," I blurted out.

Silence resounded in the wake of my confession, and I tensed, not wanting to look up.

"I know," Mom said, her voice gentle.

I lifted my head to meet her gaze. Her eyes were soft and a little sad, but she smiled.

"Did you figure out the tattoos your father and I are getting?" she asked, nervously shifting in her seat.

"Didn't you hear me?" I asked. Why wasn't she angry? Or upset? Or addressing what I'd just admitted?

"The tattoos, August," she said, a gentle smile on her face.

"Coordinates, right?" I said, glancing over the papers I'd prepped for their appointment.

"For our home," Mom said. "The one we raised you in. No matter where we go, we'll always carry it with us."

Oh. Heat welled up in my eyes, my vision going wobbly from the liquid there. I'd been so worried Mom and Dad moving away meant more of the same, that I was too needy, too much, that they didn't care as much as I did about all the memories we'd shared in that house growing up. That with them moving, we'd lose what kept our family together.

But this gesture meant everything.

Not only were they getting the coordinates inked on them, but they were having me do it. No matter how far they went, they'd have a part of me with them. My heart squeezed tight.

"I had the feeling you didn't want to go to Florida," Mom admitted. "When you started responding to our messages less and less, that was one of the biggest tip offs."

I wiped my eyes to clear them from the glossiness and washed my hands before getting the tattoo gun prepped. "You're not mad?"

Mom shook her head. "Your dad and I want to make this move, but I can see you've carved out a beautiful life for yourself here. It was a bit of selfishness on our part wanting to drag you away from it because you're our only kid. We'll just miss you a lot."

My heart squeezed hard. That was the exact way I felt.

"I didn't want to let you down," I admitted with a hard swallow. "And before Drake and I had solidified things, I had considered the idea. So much was shifting all at once. But this place here? I don't think

I'll ever find a workplace like it again. And I know for a fact I'll never find anyone else like Drake."

"Glad to hear it." Drake's voice sounded behind me. I glanced back. He and my dad had appeared with chairs to watch Mom getting her first tattoo. Odd as fuck way for my boyfriend to meet my family, but kind of perfect in the same breath. My insides fluttered as our gazes locked, and I beamed at him, unable to contain the fierce joy flooding through me.

"You were right about August," Mom said to Dad. "Guess I'm doing dishes for the next month."

"You had a bet on it?"

"We're old, bored, and retired," Dad said. "Of course we put a bet on it. Besides, chances are, you'll get sick of seeing us. We'll be up to visit as often as possible."

"Never," I responded, and Dad reached over to ruffle my hair, as if I were still a kid, not a fully grown adult. I basked in the attention, not giving a damn it was in front of Drake. A gentle smile lingered on his lips, those dark eyes of his warm, and I loved that he'd be getting to watch me ink.

Only fair, after I'd gotten to see him fight the apartment fire. Granted, putting ink on someone versus saving lives didn't compare in the slightest. Like comparing apples to...well, maybe not oranges. Aubergines?

I prepped the tattoo gun and settled into the seat. "You're getting the forearm, right?"

"Yes," she said. "Be gentle on this old lady."

I rolled my eyes. She wasn't that old. "Either you'll have a pain tolerance for it, or you won't, but we can take as many breaks as needed."

"Ready?" I asked as I turned on the machine and the gun hummed in my hand.

Mom was squeezing her eyes shut, teeth gritted. "Sure."

I shook my head, a grin on my lips and my heart light as I set to work.

***

Both Mom and Dad had howled the entire tattoo appointments, but they survived the process, owners of fresh ink. I gave them each a huge hug and promised to meet them at the restaurant, which was the original plan. Drake had cracked jokes with my folks the entire time, blending in like he'd known them for years, rather than just meeting them. I loved every second of seeing him with them.

"Ready to go?" I asked Drake, who was chilling back and skimming through his phone while I sterilized the last of my equipment. He'd tried to help a few times, ended up contaminating things, and we'd agreed I was better off finishing the job up myself.

"Hell yes," he said. "I'm starving."

"Tell me about it," I said, then looked up. His eyes gleamed, a wolfish grin on his lips. Heat bloomed between us, but we didn't have enough time for a quickie. "Stop. Now. I refuse to sit through dinner with a boner."

"Who has a boner?" Rory said, strolling into the room. "Don't let me stop you."

"That's definitely stopping us," Drake commented. He'd gotten used to Rory at once, and I loved seeing how he slotted into my life like he'd always been there. Every other relationship had involved more of a struggle or getting blindsided when I found out they weren't as interested as me, but with Drake, he met my energy every step of the way.

"We've got dinner with my folks," I said, packing away the last of the tools and rinsing my hands again.

"Did you tell them?" Rory asked, crossing his arms as he leaned against the wall.

"They'd already figured out," I said. "Apparently I don't hide things well."

Rory barked out a laugh at the same time Drake said, "No."

I shook my head, warmth welling in my chest. I'd rather people know me than feel misunderstood. And these people knew me better than anyone. I clapped a hand on Rory's shoulder. "Thanks for the push though."

Rory met my gaze. "Any time."

Drake slipped up beside me and linked his hand in mine. "Let's get out of here."

The press of our palms together ignited the electricity inside me, and I reveled in the feel of it. We strode past Cas's stall where he was hunched over, working intently on a sketch, past Nyx's empty one, since she'd gone home to her girlfriend, Becky.

When we exited Alchemy Ink, the night sky greeted us.

Already, velvet dark stole over the landscape, the slight chill to the air caressing me. I paused for a moment and stared at the skyline. Kennett Square spread out before us, a small town that I'd carved my mark on from an early age. Headlights flashed by from the cars passing us on the road, but trees carved their silhouettes in every direction.

"A little surreal, right?" Drake murmured at my side, his palm still in mine.

That encapsulated how I felt perfectly.

Right now, I stood hand in hand with the man I was certain I'd someday marry.

And my past, my present, and my future rushed around me in such an intense swirl I couldn't help but get caught up in it.

My dreams had always been simple ones. Chase after the art I loved. Find someone to spend the rest of my days with.

And now, standing in front of Alchemy Ink with Drake? My dreams had merged into one beautiful picture I couldn't wait to paint.

Together, we'd chase after a lifetime of color, one stroke on the page at a time.

Epilogue

Drake

Three Months Later...

The day of the fundraiser had arrived.

Now that it had come, I was excited, but I no longer placed the weight on it that I once had. Back then, I'd been searching for a way to stand out, to feel like I'd achieved something with my life. I'd been aimless and searching for a direction.

And in the process, I'd found everything I'd been looking for in one person.

August had been over my apartment every waking second since we started dating, with occasional bouts at his place, and I couldn't wait until his lease was up.

I was absolutely asking him to move in.

We might be zooming ahead at lightning speed in our relationship, but I'd spent enough time dancing around people who hadn't understood me and never would. August made me feel complete in a way I'd craved my entire life.

"You ready to raise some money in style?" August asked, driving us toward the firehouse. He'd offered to be the designated driver tonight, since I would need to drink, or twenty, once we got there.

"Don't know about style. I'm pretty sure I'll get there and no one will show up." I scrubbed my palms across my face as August flew down the street, far too close to the firehouse for my liking. I needed a dozen extra days to prepare. The emails had been sent, the equipment hauled in, tickets sold, but there were still so many small loose threads involved with even a one-night show. Yet I hadn't been alone through the process.

"Harmonica Joe will for sure bring in randoms," August said. "He has a weird little cult entourage in the area."

No lie there. We'd gone to a few other oddball shows to scout talent and settled on him to open. But with the weight of funds for our firehouse's new kitchen on the line, as well as not wanting to waste the time of people I respected, my nerves were at an all-time high.

The familiar sight of the firehouse didn't calm me like it usually did. August drove around back to park, and I noted the space to the side of the building we'd cleared for the show. Thank fuck it wasn't raining. If the sky had opened up, we would've been screwed, trying to cram the whole show inside the firehouse.

Once we parked, I hopped out and started striding to the front. August thankfully kept pace with me, which was a feat in my anxiety-ridden state.

Already, the cones were set up to block off certain areas, half of the initial setup work done.

I blinked and blinked again.

August clapped a hand on my shoulder. "We had some early help."

"Hey, he finally arrived," Serena called from where a few familiar faces were over by the platform we were using for the stage. Mom, Dad, Blair... all my family members were here. And not just them. August's parents were milling around the side of the building, busy setting up signage. Dooley and Jacobs were shuffling a few bigger pieces of equipment out.

My heart thumped hard, like it'd burst right out of my chest.

"I know you and the crew at the firehouse have this handled, but we wanted to help too," August said. "Folks from my work will be coming to offer help soon too. They're all excited for the show, especially Cas."

I leaned in to August and pressed a kiss to his lips. I knew exactly who had set this into motion.

Gratitude spread in my chest—for him, for our family and friends, for the life we were building together.

Everything was better with August Jones around.

When we separated, I sucked in a sharp breath. My dad approached, so I strode to meet him midway. He looked completely out of place for a punk show, wearing a salmon-colored polo with his hair tightly combed, and I loved it.

"Tell me where you want us. Your mom and I are so proud."

Those words caused my heart to squeeze tight. I'd had Mom and Dad's approval all along, and a small part of me understood that. I just needed to figure it out for myself. August's easy acceptance, the way he meshed with me like no one else had given me the push I needed more than anything in realizing that.

"Thanks," I said, clutching at my nape. Embarrassment flushed through me at how many people had shown up to help. What had seemed like a long task would be over far too easily, and it was thanks to everyone in both my corner and August's—which was a hell of a lot of people. "There are a few more signs tucked into the firehouse that I'd brought earlier. We can start there."

"Put us to work," August said, his bright grin lighting up his features.

With him at my side, I could accomplish anything.

***

"You're a great crowd," Ethan shouted from the stage, his voice echoing across the lot. And he wasn't wrong. We'd amassed a much larger group than the handful of families who attended the spaghetti dinners.

Night had fallen, but the spotlights and lighting rigs we'd set up were holding strong, and even with a few technical hiccups with the sound system, we'd had enough people jumping in to tweak things that we managed to make it work. Chief had pulled me aside to thank me profusely for the turnout for the fundraiser, and damn, I brimmed with pride. Not only had a lot of family and friends shown up for the concert, but a lot of the clientele at Alchemy Ink had been interested too, and a younger crowd had turned up, including the fans of both Spring Fires and Harmonica Joe. Altogether, the energy tonight was electric.

Mom and Dad hung back from part of the crowd, probably to avoid getting caught up in it, but they were deep in conversation with August's parents, which I loved to see. Chief and his family and a lot of the other older folks lingered around the back, drinking a beer and watching from a distance.

Serena and Blair were both giving Dooley far too much attention—the man didn't need any ego stroking. And the entire Alchemy Ink crew had filtered in. Cas and Rory were a few feet from us, along with Jacobs, and we'd been thrashing to the latest song with them. And Nyx and Becky hung back a little farther, watching the show with Owen and Wyatt.

August and I were drenched in sweat. After Harmonica Joe's eclectic but fun set and the energy from Spring Fires, we'd been dancing with the rest of the crowd. It was all bodies and chaos and the sort of vibe I adored with all my favorite people.

"We were going to perform our song Fire Alarm, but considering we're performing for a bunch of firefighters, we had the notion this wasn't the right crowd to be screaming 'fire' around."

Laughter burst out from the audience, and damn, I was having such a blast. I thought I'd be a nervous mess by now, but instead, I was just enjoying myself, surrounded by the best people in the world and next to my favorite person.

"So, we're going to launch into a crowd favorite instead," Ethan called, and the drummer let out a little drill on the set. "Who's ready for Pomegranate Memories?"

The crowd erupted in sound, so different from the sirens that usually burst from this place. Seeing my home away from home transformed into this concert was another personal thrill. I loved the firehouse, loved the crew here, and I couldn't imagine a more perfect place for this.

All the better that we'd raised enough for a kitchen remodel and then some.

August leaned in, his lips brushing against my ear. "Reminds me of our first concert together."

A shiver raced through me. That night would be emblazoned in my mind for the rest of my life, the first moment where I got the inkling that he might be the one.

I fell in love with the boy at the punk show.

That teenage daydream of mine had seemed so unlikely back then, but everything about meeting August, falling for him, felt a little bit like fate.

And I'd hold on to what I'd found with all my might, chasing after each new adventure with him by my side.

Afterword

Thank you for reading August and Drake's story, the start of the Alchemy Ink series!

I love this cozy Hot Under the Collarverse, and I can't wait to bring you more stories in this universe, starting with this one. While it began with Hot Under the Collar and headed into the Brannon Boys, now to Alchemy Ink, the low-angst, ridiculous romps have been so much fun, and I'm enjoying every escape into their world.

I've been burning to write a tattoo shop series for a long time now, and I'm so excited to spend more time at Alchemy Ink and with my latest group of queer found family here. They're such a wonderful group, all colorful and artistic, and I love getting to still see plenty of Rory as well. The next one in the series is featuring our prickly ginger, Caspian, and his background is so fascinating.

If you enjoyed the book, leave a review. Kind words are what us authors survive on, and I can tell you personally I treasure each and every one.

Want the latest updates on my books? Best way is to join my reader group, Katherine McIntyre's Mayhem, or my newsletter!

Also by

Coming next in the Alchemy Ink series is Caspian's book, Stroke Frequency!

One wild convention with a hottie cosplayer turns into Caspian's worst nightmare—marriage.

Caspian

The point of this Vegas Comic Con trip is to unwind, enjoy myself, and steer clear of commitments—especially anything serious. A deadbeat dad and divorce debt sealed my opinion on marriage early on. So when I meet a gorgeous-as-hell cosplayer at the bar who's on the same light-and-easy wavelength as me, my trip's about to get even better.

Levi

One blackout drunk night in Vegas should've been just that, but when I get home, I find out...I accidentally got married. A quick search nets me the discovery that not only is the guy I met in Vegas on the East Coast like me...but he lives less than an hour away.

When I surprise him at work, we both agree that getting a divorce is first thing on the agenda. Should be easy, right?

However, between flaky lawyer hurdles, accidental Mom meetings, and a fake-real?-husband drop-in at my shitty sister's baby shower, I end up falling head over heels in love with him.

Yet Caspian's terrified of remaining married, and I'm terrified of what happens when this ends.

Also by

Want hurt/comfort romances featuring a geeky, queer found family? Read across the rainbow with the Dungeons and Dating series!

Strength Check (Dungeons and Dating #1)

Wisdom Check (Dungeons and Dating #2)

Intelligence Check (Dungeons and Dating #3)

Constitution Check (Dungeons and Dating #4)

Dexterity Check (Dungeons and Dating #5)

Charisma Check (Dungeons and Dating #6)

Or if you want your hurt/comfort romances kinkier, check out the Leather and Lattes series!

Immersion Play (Leather and Lattes #1)

Extraction Play (Leather and Lattes #2)

Percolation Play (Leather and Lattes #3)

Filtration Play (Leather and Lattes #4)

Concentration Play (Leather and Lattes #5)

Also by

If you're looking for light kink, high heat, and low angst, dip your toes into my other universe...Hot Under the Collar, filled with geeks, bears, and blue collar workers.

Sweat Connection (Hot Under the Collar #1)
Hot Conduit (Hot Under the Collar #2)
Joint Penetration (Hot Under the Collar #3)

And if you enjoyed the folks in Hot Under the Collar, then you'll love the spinoff into Ollie's family with The Brannon Boys!

Heat Transfer (Brannon Boys #1)
Bond Strength (Brannon Boys #2)
Direct Nailing (Brannon Boys #3)

Also by

If you're a fan of fairytale retellings featuring monsters, found families, and falling for the villain, check out the Monstrous Cravings series:

The Thorn and the Spire (Monstrous Cravings #1)
The Beacon and the Brine (Monstrous Cravings #2)
The Adder and the Ally (Monstrous Cravings #3)

About the author

Katherine McIntyre is feisty with a big attitude despite their short stature. They write stories featuring snarky women, ragtag crews, and men with bad attitudes—high chance for a passionate speech thrown into the mix. As a genderqueer geek who's always stepped to their own beat, they've made it their mission to write stories that represent the broad spectrum of people out there. Easily distracted by cats and sugar.